RASCAL

A Dog and His Boy

RASCAL
A Dog and His Boy

KEN WELLS

illustrations by
CHRISTIAN SLADE

Alfred A. Knopf 🐎 New York

THIS IS A BORZOI BOOK PUBLISHED BY ALFRED A. KNOPF

Visit us on the Web! www.randomhouse.com/kids
Educators and librarians, for a variety of teaching tools, visit us at
www.randomhouse.com/teachers

Library of Congress Cataloging-in-Publication Data
Wells, Ken.
Rascal : a dog and his boy / by Ken Wells ; illustrated by Christian Slade. —1st ed.
p. cm.
ISBN 978-0-375-86652-4 (trade) — ISBN 978-0-375-96652-1 (lib. bdg.) —
ISBN 978-0-375-89645-3 (e-book)
1. Beagle (Dog breed)—Fiction. 2. Teenage boys—Fiction. 3. Human-animal relationships—Fiction.
4. Louisiana—Fiction. I. Slade, Christian, ill. II. Title.
PS3573.E4923R37 2010
813'.54—dc22
2009037606

The text of this book is set in 12-point Goudy.

Printed in the United States of America
September 2010
10 9 8 7 6 5 4 3 2 1

First Edition

For Lisa, Sara, and Becca

Chapter 1

My name is Rascal, and the boy I got says I might be the happiest dog that God ever let live.

Maybe I am!

I used to live up at Voclain's Farm, but I don't no more and I'm glad I don't.

Nonc Noon Voclain gave me away. He don't miss me. I chased his chickens, though I never caught one, and he chased me for chasin' 'em.

He ain't too spry, Nonc, so he never caught me, though Tante Lo-Lo, his wife, once swiped me with the broom bristle.

Some dogs woulda run off mad or scared, but I just run off laughin'.

I'm a sweet dog. I *am*. I don't think I got the bite in me. Even for them rabbits I chase.

But oh boy, do I chase 'em!

Anyway, I wadn't the onliest dog around. Nonc's got him *beaucoup* dogs, a whole jambalaya of dogs, but he ain't so good at dogs. Me, I'm still just a pup, and I already know Nonc ain't no real dog man.

Not like the boy I got me now. He's a real dog boy. He smells good. He knows what a dog's about.

See, Nonc would feed us on slops he picks up from the schoolhouse and chicken bones and leftovers from the gumbo pot, and them turnips that he won't eat, no matter how many different ways Tante Lo-Lo fixes 'em.

Now, a dog will eat most anything and be glad he ate it, but turnips?

I'm with Nonc on that one.

And if you get them chicken bones crossways in your throat, uhn-uhn. *Uhn-uhn!*

Momma, 'fore she got run over on the shell road by that sugarcane truck, said, "You watch them bones, Rascal!"

Problem is, a dog, when he's hungry, don't watch nuttin'.

Ole Babette Redbone choked on a chicken bone last winter. The dogs said she danced 'round in a big circle with her eyes all bugged out, and then she run smack into the cistern post and died.

Sad!

Nonc did throw her a nice dog funeral, though. He even got the priest to come sprinkle water on the grave—I'm not lyin'. 'Course, she'd chased a lotta coons for that man. What he did was only right.

Tante Lo-Lo, she fixes her gumbo heavy with cayenne pepper, and ain't a dog and pepper ever got along. Even Nonc gets red-faced after he eats that gumbo. He runs around the backyard fannin' hisself with his hands, pantin' and yellin', "Lawd, 'Ti' Claude, woman, you catchin' me a heart attack wit' that pepper! Ai-yi-yi!"

You'd think he'd stop eatin' that gumbo, but there's no accountin' for people and the things they do.

Anyway, a dog pretty much eats what's there, and there's a lot of leftover gumbo around Voclain's Farm. But after you eat it, you either barkin' all night or you eatin' grass all the next day.

A dog don't eat grass 'cause he *likes* it.

The onliest one who don't bark is Tubby LeBasset. He's about the onliest dog who don't get the gripe after eatin' Tante's leftovers. He's got a stomach hard as a black-iron syrup pot. He once drug a dead muskrat in the yard that had laid in the bayou for a couple of days. The garfish had already chewed on it and spit it out. The turtles—same thing. Wouldn't no other dog come close to it but Tubby; him, he ate on it all day, gnawed it down to the bones, then gnawed the bones down to the nub.

After he was done, he licked hisself proud and satisfied all over.

When the buzzards come in the yard to get the rest, they didn't even get a snack.

You ever seen anything uglier than a buzzard? I ain't.

Now that I've moved away to my boy, who stays at Miz Henrietta's place, I miss Tubby, just like I miss Momma. I miss a lot of the dogs, and that big ole cat. But a dog ain't never gonna spend too much time bein' sad and lonesome. That ain't what a dog's about.

A dog's about runnin' and chasin' and eatin' and barkin'. And love, love, love!

The other thing about Tubby is that he's about the onliest dog in the Voclain yard who ain't afraid of Big Maw. Tubby's too fat to be afraid of nuttin', I guess. Fattest beagle on this bayou, Nonc says. Maybe in Loosiana.

Nonc says Tubby ain't worth nuttin' chasin' rabbits, and it's true he don't muss hisself up runnin' hard, though he can smell up them rabbits good as the next beagle. Nonc says he keeps Tubby 'cause Tubby's purebred—he got pure blood—and he wants him to spread that pure blood around. He bought Tubby from somethin' called a kennel way up in Tennessee and paid good money for him bein' purebred. Tubby's blood is so pure it's registered someplace.

Tubby come in a fancy crate on the Greyhound bus, everybody says. He ain't no low-down Cajun *bayou* dog sneakin' in from the junkyard.

He talks funny, he does. Twangy and such. He says "howdy" and "gosh durn."

Tubby does like them lady dogs. Now and then, Nonc puts Tubby in a chicken wire pen with them lady dogs and they go rasslin' 'round. They carry on like they're havin' fun.

I 'spect they are!

I seen him and Momma in there one time.

Momma told me Tubby is my daddy, though Tubby ain't ever said such to me. Maybe he don't know it. A pup is always closer to his momma than his daddy anyway. But he likes me. He woulda give me some of that muskrat he dragged in the yard had I wanted some.

I said no thank you.

I was startin' to tell you 'bout Big Maw.

Even Bon-Bon and Mamou, them long-legged deer dogs, don't mess with Big Maw. Of course, them dogs don't have nuttin' to do with nobody, much less some mean ole cat.

What is it about long-legged deer dogs that make 'em so stuck-up, ehn?

OK, they can run fast, true, and they bark loud and deep as a tugboat horn. But have they actually ever *caught* a deer?

No, same as I ain't never *caught* a rabbit. Now, I don't *wanna* really catch me no rabbit. But I think they *really* wanna catch a deer, and they always mad that they ain't caught one yet.

Nonc goes out with Bon-Bon and Mamou, and he shoots *at* them deer while them hounds go runnin' and barkin' their fool heads off and scarin' the gumbo out of them poor deer. But Nonc ain't never caught him no deer, neither.

He don't see good, Tante says. She says, "You blind as a baby possum, Noon! Only way you'll ever shoot a deer is if you give the gun to the deer and let 'em shoot their fool selves!"

Nonc says, "I'm not blind, woman! I see good as the next man!"

She says, "That's if the next man is a blind man! Get you some huntin' glasses, beb!"

He says, "Like I tole you, woman, God ain't never gonna catch me in no huntin' glasses!"

She says, "Well, then God ain't never gonna catch you wit' no deer, neither! Catch me some venison, *chèr*!"

Maybe Bon-Bon and Mamou are stuck-up 'cause Nonc don't feed 'em leftovers. He goes to town and buys 'em that store-bought food that comes in a burlap sack and smells like warm chickens when you mix it with water. Even Tubby don't get such food, even though he's got pure blood.

Them deer dogs stand over in the shade of the big oak tree and eat that store-bought food like they at the kitchen table, serious. Don't ax for a bite—they'll bite you.

Funny thing about Big Maw—me and that lady get along. She'd tore up five or six dogs already before I was ever born. Gonna tear up a few more, I 'spect.

I run into her before I knew I was s'posed to be scared. Momma never told me not to go over there. I have four brothers and two sisters, and Momma was tired all the time, feedin' and runnin' around after everybody. I could go where I pretty much wanted to.

Big Maw lives out in Nonc Noon's barn raisin' her babies and givin' them rats a fit.

Well, she used to give them rats a fit. Till she ate 'em all.

Everybody thinks rats are smart, but I'm not so shore. Every rat on this bayou knows 'bout Big Maw, but a few still come sneakin' 'round tryin' to move into the barn. I don't really blame 'em. The barn's nice. All the dogs say it's a shame the cats have took it over 'cause it's dark and cool in the summer and warm in the winter. A dog could be real happy sleepin' in the shade in the hot weather or snugglin' up in all that hay in the cold.

Ain't no house dogs on Voclain's Farm. Most everybody else sleeps under the long front porch.

One day, after I'd met Big Maw, I saw a young rat sneakin' along Nonc's fence line.

I said, "Where you goin'?"

"The barn."

"I wouldn't if I was you—bad ole cat in there."

He looked at me crossways. He said, "As if I'd listen to a dog."

See what I mean about rats? I was just tryin' to help the fella out.

I didn't say nuttin' back.

He got ate the next day. I saw Big Maw chewin' on him myself, her and her babies. His tail was stickin' out of a kitten's mouth.

I couldn't feel too bad about it, neither.

Before I knew about Maw, I went in the barn one day 'cause a dog wants to go everyplace sooner or later. It ain't just cats that are curious. I saw them kittens and I didn't mind. Kittens smell good, too. I smelled them and they smelled me.

We were smellin' away. Rubbin', too. Oh yeah!

Next thing I know there's this cat just lookin' down at me from a bale of hay. Big ole cat. Way bigger'n me. Biggest cat you'll ever see. Gray and white.

Whiskers like a broom bristle.

She had scary yellow eyes, big as egg yolks.

She said, "No dogs allowed in this barn."

"Uh, I didn't know that."

She said, "Who's your momma?"

"Blanche Naquin. She come from Naquin's Farm down the bayou."

She said, "Well, she ain't the worst dog."

"No, ma'am, she ain't."

"Now, look at you—polite."

"Yes, ma'am."

She said, "What you think of cats?"

I said, "I guess I don't mind 'em, what I know of 'em. I don't know much yet."

She said, "Hah, most dogs don't know much, ever!"

She said, "What cats smell like?"

I said, "They smell some like dogs, and a bit like flowers."

"Mee-oww!" she said. "Listen to you!"

She looked at me good, but them big ole yellow eyes went soft. "OK, you can play wit' my kitties, but no rough stuff. I know how you dogs are. And don't come over here too often 'cause I don't want them other dogs to think Maw's got soft."

"No, ma'am."

She said, "I'll be watchin' you good. I got these."

She showed me her claws. They was big and sharp.

"And these."

She showed me her teeth. They was white and pointy, though one was broke off.

She saw that I noticed that.

"Oh, that one. That one's in a dog someplace."

She said, "You know, all dogs turn out bad sooner or later."

I said, "Uhn-uhn, that's not what Momma says."

She looked at me cockeyed and said, "What is it your momma says?"

"She says I gotta grow up to be a good dog."

Big Maw smiled the way cats do. "You'd be the first one," she said.

I said, "What about Tubby LeBasset? He's got pure blood."

"Shuh, *him*? He act high-tone but he's a lazy good-for-nuttin', is what he is. Well, maybe he's funny. I might give him that much. He might not be the worst dog, neither."

I didn't tell her she was talkin' 'bout my daddy.

I played for a while, me and two of them li'l cats. Boozoo and Doopsie, they're called. We run and rolled around. They scratched me some, but I didn't bite 'em, not even playful. Not with that lady watchin' me.

Boozoo bit my ear twice, but not hard. Doopsie bit my tail, same way. I didn't mind.

I like rasslin'. Cats, dogs, don't matter. I might even rassle a rabbit if a rabbit would sit still long enough.

I guess I wouldn't rassle no possum. Or a coon. The dogs say possums stink, plus they fall over dead if you look at 'em crossways. What fun is that?

And coons rassle dirty. Coons will roll over and razor up a dog's belly with them back feet of theirs.

Mean!

Later, I axed Momma about that cat.

She said, "Oh, did you go in the barn?"

I said, "Yes, ma'am."

"Maw has an excitable nature. You have to be careful around her."

"You mean she bites?"

"She can do worse than bite. Most dogs make her nervous. Of course, some dogs make *me* nervous."

"Does Tubby make you nervous?"

"Whatever do you mean, Rascal?"

I shrugged. "I dunno. Just axin'. I see the way you act 'round him sometime. Kinda jumpy."

Momma just smiled at that.

She said, "Alida would never hurt a pup, though she might chase one off."

"Who's that?"

"That's Big Maw's real name."

"Y'all friends?"

"We talk. Woman talk. It's just the way of the world with dogs and cats. Some of us get along, but most of us don't. It's always been that way."

When Momma got run over by that cane truck, Big

Maw come outta the barn and into the yard to see me. She walked right through the middle of all them dogs. A few slunk off to the Big Ditch to hide. Not one of 'em growled or barked at her.

I guess they knew better.

Them deer dogs acted like they didn't even see her. As if.

Big Maw said, "It's a doggone, low-down, swamp-stinkin', cat-wailin', rat-bitin' shame, Rascal. Them Cajun farmers drive them trucks too fast! Your momma wadn't the worst dog, no she wadn't."

I said, "No, ma'am, she wadn't. But I never liked her chasin' them cane trucks. I told her not to, but . . . well . . ."

Big Maw looked at me soft.

"You know, Rascal, I talked to your momma 'bout that myself one time. I told her that it wadn't a smart thing to do, and you know what she said? She said, 'I know, Alida, I know. But I hear them ole wheels growlin' on that gravel road and some-thin' just *gets in me.* I think them wheels are *alive.* I don't wanna catch them trucks—I just *gotta* chase 'em.' "

"She told you that?"

"She did, puppy. And you know, that's just how it goes sometimes. Sometimes things get aholt of us and won't let us go."

I puzzled over this for a bit, and then I said, "You mean like smellin' bunnies?"

She smiled and said, "Somethin' like that. Like me get-tin' after them rats. Rascal, I'm after a rat, I'm liable to chase it 'cross the road, who cares what's comin'. In fact, I did run across the road one time wit'out lookin'—I had a big daddy rat runnin' for the bayou. Them rats know that's the onliest chance they got if Maw's on their tail. Maw won't go swimmin'—not even for a juicy ole rat. Anyway, that big daddy rat run right under a car—and I stopped just before I got squashed by the back wheels. The only reason I didn't end up like your momma is 'cause, like you know, cats is the quickest thing there is."

"Faster than snakes?"

Big Maw stopped and looked at me, and somethin' strange come into her eyes. I saw a bit of temper there.

She looked up and shook her head.

"Rascal," she said, "do Maw a favor. Don't talk to me about snakes, OK?"

"Oh, sorry, Big Maw. I, uh . . ."

She looked at me and got soft again. She give me a li'l lick, which she ain't never done before. I ain't never been licked by a big cat, but it felt all right.

"Ain't nuttin' to it, Rascal—skeeter on a gator's nose. Listen, now don't you be mopin' around. You can come over to the barn and see my boys again. You can come play. Any ole time."

I said I would.

Nonc give Momma a good enough funeral. Built her a li'l wood box and buried her over on the bayouside by that mossy ole oak tree she used to like to snooze under in the summertime. All the dogs come by, and Big Maw and her kittens, too.

I didn't feel like visitin' them cats for days and days. I was too sad. But then I went. I figgered a dog's gotta keep bein' a dog. I went pretty often.

I come out one day and Blackie Grand Baton said, "What's wrong wit' you, ehn? What kinda dog go and hang out wit' cats all day long? Tell me that much?"

I don't say nuttin' to Blackie usually. He's a big growly dog, mostly black but splotchy in places. Half Catahoula cur dog, the other dogs say. He hunts them nootras, though. That's why Nonc keeps him.

The dogs say nootras is about all Nonc really catches 'cause they're stupid and slow and they all over the place and they smell like sour mud.

A blind, three-legged dog could track a nootra.

They got 'em some teeth, though. Big long things, orange as them satsumas that grow on Nonc's trees. They can slice a dog good.

Momma told me Blackie ain't really such a bad dog, but he's always grouchin' 'cause he's got worms in his guts and Nonc won't buy the worm medicine to fix him. She said Nonc's only got so much money to go 'round and he won't waste a nickel of it on a beat-up, mixed-up dog like Blackie.

She said one time Blackie went in the barn and chased after some cats and Maw come off the rafters onto his back.

He come out with about half of his right ear missin' and Maw's tooth stuck in the other part.

Blackie used to have big pointy ears that stick straight up. Now only one does.

He didn't go back there no more.

I guess I wouldn't, neither.

One day a lady come out to Voclain's Farm. I come to learn she was Miz Henrietta Lirette. She spoke proper. She kissed

Nonc on the cheek and talked 'bout how she worked at the school down the bayou. She said, "Uncle, I need a dog, a good-natured dog, preferably a pup. It's for the boy I've taken in."

Nonc said, "He hunts?"

"He does. He seems to love it."

"Coons, rabbits, or squirrels?"

"Coons some, but squirrels mostly, I think. He's always talking about the opening day of squirrel season."

Nonc looked around, squinty like he always does, and there I was. He said, "That's the one for you, beb. That *'ti'* Rascal there. He's gonna be a great huntin' dog, him. He's got good blood, too."

Now, I ain't complainin', but Nonc didn't know whether I would be a good huntin' dog or not. He'd only took me once and it wadn't serious. We just went back of them cane fields behind the farm where some alfalfa grows, me and all my brothers and sisters. We smelled us up a coupla them bunnies, and we run around chasin' and barkin'. We made plenty of noise.

Nonc didn't even bring a gun.

Them rabbits smell better than cats! Better than boys!

A dog like me catches wind of them cottontails and he goes crazy, cain't help it. I barked like I ain't never barked, and my whole body started shakin' like muscadine jelly. Ai-yi-yi!

Them rabbits run into a ditch full of dewberry bushes. I put on the brakes quick, but my sister Jolie run right in there. She didn't run long. She come out whimperin', all muddy and scratched up. She had briars stuck up all in her ears and tail. I give her a good lickin' all over. I got me a briar in my tongue, but that's what a dog does for dogs he loves.

I guess I'm closest to Jolie of all my brothers and sisters. I miss her, too. A man come and took Jolie away one day. He give Nonc twenty dollars for her. Nonc seemed to be pleased with all that money, and I was happy for Jolie.

The man seemed nice. He petted her real sweet.

Momma said you gotta watch them briar patches 'cause snakes like it in there.

Snakes and dogs don't get along a'tall.

I ain't met no snakes yet, but already I don't like 'em. The dogs say one ole hound named King got bit on the nose by a water moccasin some time ago, and his head swole up big as a water bucket 'fore he died.

The dogs say that snake—Ole Swamp—is still around here and pretty much six foot long. Big around as a cantaloupe. Fangs like the grabber on a cane knife. Got enough poison to kill two, three dogs at once.

Sneaky, too!

Anyway, I figger Nonc packed me off 'cause he already had way too many dogs and I chased his chickens, not 'cause he thinks I'm a good huntin' dog.

He told Miz Henrietta I was worth at least twenty dollars, as much as that man paid for Jolie, 'cause I was almost pureblood beagle, 'cept that Momma has some bluetick in her from her side of the family. But Nonc told the lady she could take me away for nuttin' as she was family.

I kinda like it that I'm almost pureblood, though I don't know why.

I kinda like it that I was worth twenty dollars, though Nonc give me away for nuttin'.

I kinda like that I got some bluetick in me. I like the way it sounds.

Sometimes I say it over and over again in my head—*blue-tick*.

The lady reached down and give me a pat on the head and a scratch on the ear. Her hands was soft. She smelled like flowers were growin' all over her—just about knocked me over. Then she picked me up and toted me to her place.

We drove in her car. It grumbled and shook some. I was scared, though not too scared. Kinda excited, too. I rode in the front seat and looked out the window, which was rolled down some. The wind blew my ears around. I barked a few times. Wadn't nuttin' really to bark at 'cept some skinny ole chickens peckin' in the johnsongrass along the shell road.

I just felt like barkin'!

We got to her house, and she took me inside and put me in a big ole cardboard box in a dim room. The box was so big I couldn't jump out of it. I started whimperin', which I don't like to do, but sometimes it just comes out, same as barkin'.

She come back after a bit and brought me some food just like them deer dogs eat. I didn't think I was hungry, but I guess I was. I ate it all quick.

She brought me some water, too. It was nice and cool, and I drunk a good bit of it.

She tied a ribbon 'round my neck and went away again.

I didn't like that, neither—that ribbon or bein' left alone. That ribbon scratched. But I didn't whimper too long.

I was tired and went to sleep, and next I know—there was my boy!

He was standin' over my box lookin' down at me sayin', "Oh, Miz Henrietta, could it be true? Look at him!"

And she said, "Every boy should have a dog, Meely."

He picked me up and nuzzled me good. Then we run outside. It was still daylight. He put me down and said, "C'mon, pup, let's go. Let's go runnin'!" and we just kept runnin'.

Yappin' and yappin', chasin' everything—mosquito hawks and butterflies and big fat ole chickens. He didn't care!

"Chase them ole chickens! Go on! Get 'em, pup! Get them dirty ole birds!"

Chasin' and barkin'!

He was chasin' and barkin', too! Barkin' just like a dog!

I chased one of them big ole roosters, and doggone if he didn't start chasin' me back! Big ole ugly white bird. He come at me spurs up!

I run for my boy and run right 'tween his legs.

My boy turned and give that ole chicken a shoe—*pow!*

That chicken run off cussin', oh yeah!

Ow-rooooo! I said.

My boy started *ow-rooin'*, too! He sounded just like me!

He tumbled down to the ground, and I caught up to him and licked him good all over the face.

He let me!

He laughed some more!

He flipped me over and give me a belly rub. I got so excited I started seein' bunnies!

I slept curled up in the corner of his bed that night. I wadn't s'posed to. The lady, Miz Henrietta, give me my own bed on the floor, a soft fluffy thing, store-bought.

She don't want dogs on the furniture.

But I hop up on that bed anyway 'most every night. My boy only shoos me down when Miz Henrietta is around. Sometimes he don't shoo me down at all. Sometimes I just hide under the covers so she don't see me. We'll hear her cloppin' down the hall on those wooden floors, and I'll dive right under the sheets.

She'll come in and say, "Is that dog in your bed again, Meely?"

And he'll say, "Uhn-uhn, no, ma'am. I don't know where that silly dog is."

Then they have themselves a giggle.

Maybe that lady's blind as Nonc Noon.

I like Miz Henrietta a lot. She looks at me tough sometimes, but a dog can tell she don't mean it. She's sweet on my boy.

He's sweet on her.

But he misses somebody. I know he does.

My boy axed Miz Henrietta what I was called, and she said Nonc called me a rascal, like he didn't know Rascal was my real name. My boy looked at me, and, though he didn't know me long, he said, "Oh yeah. This pup's a rascal, all right. I like that name, Rascal."

Well, I like it, too. It was Momma who named me.

And here I am. Rascal.

I wonder what them stuck-up ole deer dogs would think now.

I got me store-bought food.

And a store-bought bed.

And my very own boy.

Chapter 2

Days have come and gone. How many, a dog don't know.

Time don't mean much to a dog.

I'm still a pup, but I'm a real huntin' dog now.

It's night and the full moon's high up in the sky, yellow as a cat's eye. Twinkly stars are everywhere. It's cool and still.

Me and my boy are headed down the grassy tractor road—what Meely calls a headland—that starts up at the back of Miz Henrietta's yard. I like the soft grass under my paws. I've got my nose down on that grass, sniffin' everything. Lots of wild things have walked here, some I cain't even name. But all the scents are old.

Beagles are nose dogs—Tubby says we got the best noses of all dogs. Them deer dogs would probly argue with that.

I like the moon myself, though some dogs don't think much of it. Big Maw likes these nights with the big moon—she says that moon gets them rats to movin' around. I miss that grumpy ole cat.

We been walkin' for about an hour. Miz Henrietta told my boy she would drive us to the woods, but he wanted to walk. She worries 'bout Meely, 'bout how he likes to walk the woods at night.

She worries about snakes and such and him gettin' lost. But he's tough and knows almost everything about the woods and fields and bayous 'cause his daddy taught him good, he says.

I've decided my boy's got a lot of dog in him. Maybe he's just a two-footed dog.

A dog don't mind the dark. Dogs see good in the dark, though maybe not as good as cats. Some dogs think you can smell things better at night.

The moon's so bright now that my boy don't need his light—what he calls a bulleye that he straps 'round his cap.

He's turned it off and we go moseyin' along, me trottin' just ahead. We walk and walk and walk, the sugarcane fields pressin' in close on both sides.

Sugarcane turns the air sweet.

We come out on the shell road and cross a bridge over the bayou. I can smell the mucky water below. I hear an ole bullfrog croakin' from off on the dark bayou bank. Some crickets, too. My boy told me he eats them frogs. Maybe he'll cook me a frog one day.

After a while, we come to a place where the moon's hid from view and there's dark shadows everywhere, and I know we've reached the woods. I can see them dark trees go up and up.

My boy switches on his bulleye and says, "OK, pup, you stay close. We're gonna head on up this ridge toward Dead John's, a place Daddy used to take me. We might even find us a rabbit out here."

Just hearin' that bunny word gets me stirred up. I give him a good *ruff-ruff* and an *oow-rooo* to boot. He laughs at that.

We go on for a while, and I'm nosin' everything and everyplace and markin' up this tree and that tree. If them deer dogs at Nonc's come through these woods, they'll know I was here. I'll bet they'll be surprised.

I smell some rabbit tracks, but they're old, and some coon tracks, too. I ain't met no coons, but I just seem to know what they smell like—all beagles are born such, or at least that's what Tubby told me one time.

I hit me a possum track, and I know it the same way as I know a coon track. The scent is so warm and strong that I see it with my nose 'bout the same way a person sees a white line painted down the middle of a blacktop road.

I find myself trottin' fast, then runnin' all-out, and barkin', runnin' so hard with my nose down that I almost smack into a big ole tree.

That smell's practically burnin' right up that tree, and I jump up high as I can, bouncin' off the trunk and barkin' like a mad dog.

My boy's runnin' up behind me, yellin', "What you got there, Rascal?"

He shines his bulleye up that tree. "Well, looka there, you've treed you a possum! You bad ole huntin' dog, you— you've treed your first critter!"

I see that possum good now that my boy's got his light on him. He's just sittin' there dumb, blinkin' down at us.

I bark and growl, and my boy bends down and musses my ears good and says, "Way to go, pup. Way to go! Now, let's go on and see what else we can find."

I don't wanna leave just yet. I'm hopin' my barkin' and growlin' will make that possum fall out of the tree dead like the other dogs say happens sometimes. I'd like to see that.

But he don't. He just sits there lookin' gray and pokey as a sad ole man.

My boy walks away and whistles for me to follow.

We go on, walkin' slow and quiet. We come to a place where the woods open up. Dark mounds poke shadowy out of the ground. My boy goes to one of the mounds and sits down.

"C'mere, pup. Let's take a rest."

I trot over and look around. I sniff the air and then the ground. I hit a smell I cain't make out.

It ain't a critter smell.

Meely gives me a pat and says, "This is Dead John's, Rascal—an ole colored cemetery Daddy showed me when I was eight or nine. Not too many people know it's even out here—the woods took it over a long time ago. Daddy says it goes way back to before the Civil War and slaves are buried here. I've always liked the place, though I don't tell too many people that—some folks might take it strange that a fella likes to hang out at night in a grave-yard way out in the woods. But it ain't spooky to me. I find it peaceful and easy. When I'd come here with Daddy, I'd try to imagine what the people were like when they were alive. Slaves, what I know of 'em, had it terribly hard. But Daddy's always sayin' even people who have good lives have hard times, and even people who have hard lives can have good times. I'm just curious about 'em, I guess. I just wonder what they ate and drank and talked about. Daddy says if these ole bones could speak, a fella could hear some interestin' stories."

My boy goes quiet. I sniff the ground again, and I know what I'm smellin'.

It's them ole bones down there.

My boy switches off his light again and lays back on the mound, his hands cupped behind his head, and says, "I'm gonna count me some shootin' stars, Rascal. This time of the year, I always see a few."

I settle in at his feet. He counts soft—there's number four, that's five. . . .

I look up at the sky, too, and them stars wink like lightnin' bugs. One of them shootin' stars floats tiny and bright down the black sky, then disappears.

All this walkin's made a dog drowsy, and I find myself driftin' off.

I'm dreamin' about Momma, and in that dream she and Big Maw are talkin' 'bout me, but I cain't quite make out what they're sayin' and I feel the dream slippin' away slow, like that water that drips from the cistern nozzle at Nonc's. Then I'm awake and the woods are still and quiet, not a breath of wind, and that yellow moon's moved right over the top of us. There's a haze around it.

I hear my boy breathin' soft, and I know he's fell asleep like I did.

I get up and stretch and sniff the air—and the hackles rise on my neck. I get a whiff of somethin', somethin' strange.

Somethin's *here*.

Whatever it is, I don't like anything about it. A growl rises up in my throat and then a howl comes out of me I didn't know I had.

Suddenly my boy's up and lookin' 'round. "Whoa, Rascal, what's wrong? What you barkin' at?"

He stands and switches on his light and shines it around for a good long time.

He don't see nuttin', and a boy cain't smell everything a dog smells.

"Well, I don't see anything, pup. I wonder what you saw. That ole possum tryin' to slip by us? We got a coon slippin' 'round? A mink? Maybe that ole *roogarou*? If you treed the *roogarou*, Rascal, you and me would be the most famous dog and boy in all of Loosiana."

He laughs, but I wish he wouldn't laugh right now. It wadn't any of the things he named, I know that.

It was somethin' *bad*.

I sniff and sniff again and pick up some kind of scent way off to my left. I nose over that way.

Somethin's movin' over at the edge of the clearin'!

I bawl like a deer dog and go runnin' toward it.

At the edge of the clearin', I don't see a thing. That scent's gone.

I trot back over to my boy.

Somethin' was watchin' us.

Meely ain't worried. He stretches and yawns. "Let's head out. I think we'll go back by way of Cancienne's corn patch. We might shine us up a rabbit for you to chase—they like sittin' up on the edge of the cornfields on a warm night like this."

He bends and pats me. "Now, if we do find a rabbit, you gotta stop chasin' when I whistle you off, OK, pooch?"

We leave Dead John's, goin' a bit faster than we come. We go on and on till we leave the woods behind and hit another headland. This one ain't used much—the grass is tall and tickles my belly. That ole moon seems to trot along with us.

My boy is shinin' his light way up ahead of us. He says with that light you can often see a rabbit's eyes before you see the rest of the rabbit.

Soon he stops. He stoops down and turns to me and whispers, "Rascal, whoa, c'mere, boy."

I trot over.

He stoops down and gives me a nuzzle and says, quiet, "There's a rabbit far up ahead, sittin' at the edge of this field to our right. You wanna chase that bunny, pup? You wanna get that ole rabbit?"

I lick his face and squeal.

"Shhh, shhh. We're gonna slip into the field here and see if we can ease up the row out of sight and surprise that rabbit. OK?"

He picks me up and shoves between some tall stalks of corn and then puts me down in the row. He puts a finger up to his lips and whispers, "Now, nice and slow and quiet."

He switches off his light again. It's dark in the row.

We go creepin' slow, my boy hunched over.

I like creepin', though I'm quiverin' all over. I can tell my boy likes creepin', too.

After a bit, he motions me to stop. He gets down on his knees and then, real slow and quiet, pokes his head through some stalks and looks out.

He pokes his head back in and gets real close to me and whispers, "He's right here, Rascal. We got us a bunny right here."

He don't have to tell me that—I can smell that rabbit like he's stuck up my nose.

I bolt through them cornstalks like a dog on fire. I bawl so loud it practically scares *me*.

I 'bout knock that bunny over.

He's so surprised that he jumps straight up in the air and comes down just about on top of me.

Ooh, he smells delicious!

Then he thumps off in three big jumps, drummin' the ground with them big back feet of his.

Boy, can he jump!

We go haulin' down that headland, the bunny dodgin' left and right and skitterin' around. He ain't foolin' me. I'm right behind him. I can see his ole cotton tail bobbin' up and down bright as a bulleye.

He sees an openin' in some cornstalks and dives right into that corn row I just come out of.

I dive right in behind him.

Far off, I hear my boy yell, "Get 'im, Rascal. Get that ole rabbit!"

I bawl like a mad dog.

That rabbit jumps so high I'm thinkin' he's jumped clear out of his big ole rabbit feet.

He comes down with a thump and I'm right on his tail.

We run and we run and we run till suddenly we pop right out of that cornfield into a big open field that smells like the air does when my boy cuts the grass. That rabbit knows he's lost cover, so he starts runnin' faster than ever.

A dark line of shadows rises up ahead, and I know right away that rabbit's runnin' for the woods.

I'm losin' ground but it don't matter.

Suddenly out of nowhere I see tons of bunnies—bunnies everywhere!

Ai-yi-yi!

They're surprised to see me, too. They scatter like spooked chickens.

There's so many rabbits I cain't even tell which one I was chasin'!

I pick the closest one and bawl so loud that my dog brain rattles.

'Fore I know it, I've run this rabbit clear into the woods.

Somewhere way back behind me, I think maybe I hear a whistle. But it ain't loud and I ain't shore it's really a whistle and, oh Lordy, these rabbits have got me stirred up.

I run on 'cause there's rabbit scent all around me now, thick as peanut butter. I hear rabbits skitterin'; I see rabbits crossin' my trail every which way.

Soon I'm all run out.

I slow to a trot and then stop, pantin' hard.

I listen, but the only sounds I hear are my heart thumpin' fast and a rabbit runnin' in dry leaves far away.

I'm too tired to even bark at him.

The woods get quiet.

I listen for my boy callin' for me, but I don't hear him.

For the first time, I realize I'm turned around. I don't know how far into these woods I've run. I cain't really be shore which way is the field I come runnin' across.

I stand quiet and still and listen. I know my boy will call me soon.

I wait and wait, but I don't hear a thing.

I'm shore he's callin', I'm just not hearin'.

I look up at that old moon. Maybe he knows where I am.

But the ole moon just looks down at me. He's got nuttin' to say.

A whimper comes up in my throat. I feel lonesome. I wish I could hear my boy.

Then I think about what my boy would do. He wouldn't be too worried. He'd just sit and think about things until he could figger out what to do.

I sit and think.

I couldn'a run all that far. I just need to be calm and get my dog bearin's. I close my eyes and sit still, breathin' slow. I try to smell and listen and feel.

And then I have an idea—a fuzzy idea, but an idea—of the way I need to go.

I trot on with only the moon for company. On and on and on.

Just when I'm thinkin' I'll be trottin' on lost all night, I hit a break in the woods, and I figger out where I am—back at Dead John's, where them mounds come out of the ground.

From here, I'm pretty shore I can find my way back to the grassy road—I might even be able to pick up my boy's scent.

I trot over to the mound where Meely counted them shootin' stars, stop, and sniff.

I can smell my boy, though not strong. But I feel a lot better already.

I start to light out again—when I hear a voice behind me.

That voice sends a *frisson* down my spine clear to my tail.

It's a deep, whispery voice, and it says, "Well, look what we have here—a poor, lost puppy. A pitiful, triflin' lost li'l thang. Now, how sad is that?"

Chapter 3

A scent slams me hard.

I yelp, jump up on the mound, and whirl around. A sound boils out of me I didn't know I had.

It's a snarl.

I look toward the voice, and there he is in the pale moonlight—a snake coiled up on a tree stump not six feet away.

He's got a big, wedgy head, and the moon glints in his black, black eyes.

He slides off that stump and comes wig-wagglin' my way.

I want to snarl again, but that snarl runs from me like a rabbit.

My ears go flat and my tail starts to tuck and my body starts to quiver, and I know I've got but one chance and that's to hightail it out of here.

But I cain't run.

I'm stuck, stuck like an ant in willow sap.

I stiffen up and start to bark like mad. I bare my teeth.

The snake stops.

He raises his ugly head to look me over good and then comes slidin' slow toward me again.

I want to look away but I cain't.

I cain't breathe.

I figger I have one chance—just go for his throat. But I cain't even feel my legs.

He slithers up close, real close, and I can smell him strong now, sour as curdled milk, dead things on his breath.

He says, "Relax, dog. Relax. Ole Swamp's not gonna hurt you. You're way too big for me to eat anyway. Ole Swamp here likes newborn puppies. Tasty they are, and oh *so* easy to swallow. And anyway, I've already had supper this week—a bunny. Ooh, now what's more tender than a young rabbit? A young bunny drenched in swamp water? Have you had one yourself? I see you do like to chase after 'em. Now, the one thing I've noticed 'bout you dogs—you waste *so* much energy. All that runnin' and barkin' and carryin'-on. Why, son, how hilarious!"

I would answer if I could find my voice.

"Anyway, it's not you I'm interested in—it's your boy. Ole Swamp here don't give a leech about dogs. We'll never be friends, snakes and dogs, but we do manage to avoid one another for the most part, and when we don't? Oh, well, you run or you get bit and then you die. Pretty simple, ain't it? But now, boys—they're another thang altogether. Boys are the worst trouble that ever got made. Not that I have use for *any* Two-Footer."

He stops, lookin' me over good.

"Do you realize, dog, that it *was* paradise till *they* got here? Us snakes ran the place till them Two-Footers took over. Well, all right, we ran the low country. See, it's sorrowful to have to give up runnin' somethin' when you've run it pretty much forever. This is the thang about snakes—we've got long, long memories. Now, dogs wouldn't understand about runnin' anything. Dogs gave up a long, long time ago—sold out to the Two-Footers for a few scraps of food and a pat on the head now and then. Dogs are pathetic suck-ups. And if you want Ole Swamp's opinion, cats ain't much better—though they like to think they are."

That snake cocks his head to the side and just stares like he's starin' right through me.

With him goin' on like that, I realize I've got my legs back.

I start to ease away, hopin' he won't notice.

'Course, snakes notice anything that moves.

Swamp laughs a whispery laugh.

"Rascal, Rascal, relax, puppy. If Ole Swamp wanted to do you in, you'da been cooked as a crawfish by now. I coulda just laid tucked up under some nice, warm leaves still as that moon up there and let you walk right into me. Bit you in the jugular and *cough, cough,* you'd drop over like a frosted alligator. I didn't 'cause—even though dogs are pathetic—I kinda like you. I'm curious about you. You and that boy."

I keep backin' up slow.

"Tsk, tsk, tsk."

He slithers up right up in my face.

"I can see you're gonna make it hard. I'm just tryin' to have a talk, and you keep tryin' to run away. Now *stop it* 'fore Ole Swamp gets mad. C'mon, pup, consider this a chance for better snake-dog relations. And make eye contact. C'mon, now. Be a good sport."

I don't know much, but I already know this snake's *craque.* And he's startin' to make me mad.

"How can you like me when you don't know me?" I say. "How do you even know my name? Besides, all the dogs over at Voclain's Farm know you're a killer—that you snuck around the farm and bit one of the dogs. Everybody knows—"

I stop, thinkin' maybe I shouldn't be bringin' up the killer part.

Swamp cocks his head at a funny angle again.

"Now, hold on a minute. I know your name 'cause I heard your boy say it. And as for that dog, you have no *personal* knowledge of what happened. You're too young to remember it yourself. But, see, it was a tragic accident—tragic! Here's the thang. That dog—King they called him—wadn't the brightest pooch on the porch. 'Stedda bein' a normal dog, chasin' coons and squirrels and rabbits and such, he liked to sniff out snake lairs. He and that gimpy ole man—whatcha call him, Uncle somebody or other?"

"You mean Nonc Noon?"

"Yeah, that one. That ole man used to follow King around with a big ole stick and poke it in them lairs and try to chase us snakes out so he could put a whuppin' on us. Cuss us out loud 'fore he ever laid eyes on us. Now, that wadn't right! Imagine somebody comin' 'round your doghouse and messin' with your friends and family like that. Anyway, all snakes know that since them Two-Footers got here, a snake don't stand a chance in the open with a man. They've got sticks and guns and cane knives, and what does a snake have? Our noggins to think with and our bellies to crawl on. And us lucky ones got these."

He opens his mouth wide and shows me his fangs.

They look like pointy, milky knives in the moonlight.

My tail starts to tuck again.

"Anyway, you catch my drift. Now, one day ole King come sniffin' in my lair—I lived in a double-wide cypress stump, a nice ole place quite a bit away from that farmyard. Had it fixed up real nice with moss and cozy skins from things I'd killed. And I had me a couple lady friends in there. 'Stedda just sniffin', that dog stuck his head right in my house! Can you imagine? Well, I reared back and give him a good hiss and showed him the white of my mouth, and he jerked his head out quick. Then, next thing I know, the fool has stuck his dumb ole head in again, barkin' and bawlin' and snappin' and generally foamin' at the mouth. Uggh-lee! A snake's gotta do *somethin'*. I was just gonna give him a li'l sting on the toe—you know, teach him a lesson—but the slobberin' fool throws hisself at me as I strike and, well, *pow!* I hit him right on the nose."

Ole Swamp shakes his head. "Shuh, it was all I could do to get my stingers outta the fool 'fore he drug me outta my log. See? Just a bad accident is all it was. Unfortunate for everybody. Especially him."

I look at Ole Swamp hard. I have to say this story confuses me.

"Well, I never heard that," I say. "That's not the story the dogs tell. They say you snuck up into Nonc Noon's pasture one day and—"

He hisses at that.

"Well, *of course* that's not the story dogs tell. Dogs are pack animals—y'all stick together. A dog'll never tell the truth about a snake to another dog. C'mon, pup, get real. Anyway, it's not a moment in my life I'm particularly proud of. I'm sorry ole King's head swole up like a watermelon 'fore he fell over dead. But do you think I wanted to waste my poison on a dog? No! I coulda caught me five suppers with the stuff I pumped into him. So now I think it's time to put this behind us and move on, don't you?"

I look at him good.

You cain't tell a thing from a snake's eyes.

He inches up even closer. "Now, I wanna know all about that boy."

"Why?"

" 'Cause I'm curious is all. Now, c'mon. Tell Ole Swamp what you know."

I can see I'm not gonna get out of this. I don't *want* to tell him about my boy. Not one thing. Maybe I can change the subject.

"Well, can I ax you somethin' first?"

"Depends."

"Is it really true snakes used to be in charge of this swamp?"

"Well, not just this swamp, son. We pretty much ran the whole shootin' match down here."

"I thought bears did."

He hisses. "Bears? Ha-ha! You ever met you a bear?"

"No."

"They're boneheads, every one of 'em—all teeth and stomach and swagger. But ain't one of 'em got a lick of sense. Big and dumb as stumps. You dogs look like geniuses compared with bears."

"What about bobcats?"

"C'mon, son, get real. There ain't never been enough bobcats around here for them to be in charge. Plus, face it, they're just overgrown barn cats. And how could cats run anything? You get three cats together and you get seven opinions on everything."

I would tell him about Big Maw runnin' the barn, but I don't think it would do any good.

"Deer?"

Swamp hiss-laughs again. "Deer? Deer, son, are sissies. I've seen *birds* spook deer right out of their skins. Now, you said you had one question, but you've already asked a gumbo pot of 'em. Let's move on!"

"I think alligators run the swamp. That's what all the dogs say."

Swamp really hisses at this. "Alligators? They're just big, fat, lazy lizards. If their brains was eggs, you could round up a dozen of them and not have enough to scramble. And, anyway, ain't so easy to find alligators these days. Them Two-Footers have took care of them, too. Most of the bull gators that used to swim around out in these sloughs are over in the shoe store now. Haw-haw."

The thing is, that *is* kinda funny, but I ain't laughin' at no snake joke.

"Maybe that's funny to you," I say, "but I've never heard the dogs say snakes ran the swamp. And I don't know how you could run things when you're, well, well . . . uh—"

"Well, *what*, dog? C'mon, spit it out."

"Well, when you're so low to the ground."

Swamp cocks his head again, like he's got to think about this.

I've stumped *him* for a second.

"Oh, right, I see—stoopin' to insult, are we?"

I look up and think maybe I've said too much when Swamp pulls his head back slow—the way a snake might 'fore he strikes.

My tail starts to tuck again. I close my eyes and wait for them stingers.

"No, no," Swamp says. "No closin' your eyes. Now look at this. Now. C'mon, I mean it. *Look* at me."

I open my eyes and yelp—Swamp's raised hisself up so that about a third of him is off the ground. His wedgy head is hoverin' right over me.

"See, dog? I can be taller than you when I wanna be. I could look them big ole deer dogs in the eye if I cared to. We ain't *always* so low to the ground. And, anyway, that's not the point. A critter don't have to have legs or be six foot tall to get the lay of the land, if you know what I mean. Now, try not to insult me anymore. You don't want to make Ole Swamp here mad. You don't."

I hear myself sayin', "No, sir, I don't."

"That's more like it."

Ole Swamp lets hisself down slow and easy. He opens his mouth wide. It's big and milky white, but his fangs are tucked back. I guess that's a good sign.

It's like he's readin' my mind.

"Right, pup, that was a yawn. Like I said, I ain't gonna bite you—as I tried to tell you about bitin' that dog, a smart snake never wants to waste his poison. It's as precious to a snake as a bone is to a dog. Now—about that boy."

I'm too frazzled to argue anymore.

"He's the first one I've had, and I ain't had him that long. He's a good boy. Good with dogs—well, he's good with me, at least. He's smart. I've taught him quite a few tricks since I moved in, like throwin' sticks. He likes to chase things, just like me—chickens and such. We rassle 'round. He don't mind bein' licked. He even licked me once on the face. He likes to hunt. Tonight we were just ramblin' and I started chasin' bunnies and, well, uh, I, uh—"

Swamp gives one of them hiss-laughs again. "Lemme guess. You ran off and let your nose get the best of your head, which is what you dogs are always doin', and you ran way too far. Then you got yourself turned around out here in the dark, and your boy just walked off and left you all alone in the woods 'cause, even though you think he's good with dogs, them Two-Footers actually don't care for nothin' but themselves."

"That's not true! He told me to listen for his whistle, and I know he whistled, but, uh, well, I had one of them bunnies close, and, uh—"

"Yeah, yeah, yeah. It's the same ole sad dog story. With you dogs, it's nose first or stomach first or snooglin' first. A dog's wired so that the very last thang he ever uses is the thang he needs the most—his head."

"Not true."

" 'Course it's true."

"No, it ain't."

"Of course it is."

"No, it ain't. And anyway, what's snooglin'? I ain't never—"

Swamp gives a big ole hiss–belly laugh.

"Snooglin'? C'mon, pup, hasn't your momma taught you nothin'?"

"My momma's taught me a lot," I say, feelin' myself get- tin' riled up. "She, uh—she—"

"Your momma's what? Your momma—"

I cut him off. "You don't know everything there is to know about dogs! You don't know a pea brain's worth about dogs. You, well, you're—"

I'm so mad I'm sputterin'.

"Well, well, now. We've got us a temper, do we? Look, I'm not actually tryin' to insult you or your dear ole momma, but I know all I need to know. You bein' here is proof. If you'da used your head, you wouldn't be stuck out here in the middle of no place with me, now would ya? You'd be home by now, sleepin' in your doghouse."

"Shows what a snake knows. I don't have no doghouse. I sleep inside the house, with my boy. I, uh—"

"Do you, now? Well, isn't that fancy? And do you take your supper at the kitchen table, too?"

"No, I got me a bowl over in the corner of the kitchen. I've got me some store-bought food and everything. I've got—"

Swamp stops me. "See, that's another thing that's wrong with dogs. You take the man's food, and it makes you lazy and stupid."

I'm lookin' at this snake, and I realize I don't know what to say. I'd like to take a bite out of him just to make him shut up.

Instead, I say, "Oh, like snakes are so smart. You spend your whole life slidin' 'round in the mud on your bellies and creepin' 'round where you don't belong and bitin' innocent dogs and eatin' poor baby chicks that never did a thing to you! You even said you eat puppies!"

He hisses at that. "Did I, now? Well, I guess I left out kittens. I eat kittens, too. Does that make you feel better? I wouldn't want you to think it's somethin' personal 'gainst dogs."

I hear another growl rise up in me.

Swamp bends his head funny again. "Well, now looka there, fire in them puppy eyes! Ain't you somethin'. Just don't do anything foolish, son, 'cause I really don't wanna hurt you. Anyway, you're *way* outta line here. Nature made us snakes just about perfect—smooth and low to the ground and quiet and efficient. Now, I'm not sayin' the average snake is a genius, but we got patience, and we know huntin' ain't just about bawlin' and makin' noise so them Two-Footers can pretend they're havin' fun. And, anyway, a snake's gotta make a livin' same as every other thang. We gotta eat, too. If you dogs were still wild and had to get your own supper now and then, you'd know what I'm talkin' about."

I look at him hard again. I wanna say somethin', but what's really terrible is that I'm stumped.

"What, cat got your tongue? Haw-haw!"

I just shake my head. I suddenly realize how tired I am. "I don't wanna talk to you no more. I, uh—"

Swamp suddenly hisses—a hiss I ain't heard before.

"Quiet," he says in a whispery breath. "Shhh, puppy, shush."

He rears up again, and a chill goes through my body. But he's lookin' behind me, starin' hard with those empty eyes. He peers out for a good, long minute, then says in another low whisper, "You need to run, dog. You need to run out of these woods and keep runnin' till you're clear."

"You mean I can go?"

"Yes, you've gotta go. Run, dog—run now!"

I wonder if this is some kind of trick, but there's somethin' strange in his voice.

He don't have to tell me twice.

I bolt straight ahead, my heart flutterin' like a bird flushed from a tree at night. I hit a path, maybe a deer trail, that slices through the tall trees, and I pick up a dark shadow on my right.

Another snarl springs up in me.

But before I can get it out, I hear that snake's whispery voice again. "That's it, dog, you fly. Swamp's gotta drop back now, but listen to what I'm tellin' you. I ain't the only big snake out here with stingers, and I ain't the only thang that don't like Two-Footers. You and your boy—y'all better be careful, you hear me?"

I just keep runnin'. I run and run and run, till I think I cain't run another step, and then I run some more.

And then, when I know I've run myself out, when I'm about to drop, when I don't care no more if there's a snake or ten behind me with their fangs all cocked ready to sink them into my rump, I've run clear out of the woods into a field of sweet alfalfa.

I sniff the air to see what my nose can tell me.

I catch lots of scents—clover, bunnies, maybe some ole spooked deer in the distance. But I catch somethin' else far off—somethin' familiar.

Suddenly it hits me.

I know where I am!

In the distance I see a tree line—the tree line that marks the edge of Nonc Noon's back pasture. I look behind me to make sure no snakes are creepin' 'round, then head that way.

Chapter 4

I come walkin' up slow through Nonc's back pasture. The first light of mornin' is creepin' into the sky. Nonc's mean ole red bull, Hurricane, stands grazin' in a corner. He's been known to chase a dog or two. He raises his big ugly head, sniffs the air, then goes back to chompin' grass. His cows are down the way a bit, flickin' their tails.

They're dull and slow and don't even look up.

It's a big ole long pasture, and halfway up it, I spy the barn. One of the two big double doors is open a crack.

I'm whupped. I just wanna sleep.

I trot over and nose into the barn.

It's cool and dark, and the air smells sweet with hay. I can already feel what it'll be like to curl up in a soft ole bale.

I don't get two feet when I'm knocked flat.

Suddenly I'm on my back—there's somethin' hunched over me, all teeth and growls and spittle.

I yelp out, "No, please, don't! It's me, Rascal! No!"

Big Maw's face, all twisted, hovers over me. Her back is hunched up and her right paw's pulled back ready to swipe me good.

Her claws look like the spurs on a rooster.

Her yellow eyes grow wide.

"Rascal?" she says. "Rascal, what in the sugarcane you doin' creepin' 'round Maw's barn this time of day? Don't you know what happens to dogs who come sneakin' 'round here?

45

Ain't just dogs. Nuttin' better come creepin' 'round Maw's place that ain't invited."

"I'm sorry, Big Maw, I wadn't thinkin'. See, I was out huntin' bunnies with my boy and we got separated and I got lost and I was stumblin' 'round the woods all night and I got waylaid by this big ole, uh— See, what happened was I got stuck with this, uh—"

I stop. I remember what Maw told me long ago about not talkin' snakes around her. I don't care to rile her up again.

She looks at me deep. "You got stuck with what, puppy?"

"I cain't say, Maw. It ain't a thing you like to talk about."

Her big ole eyes get slitty. Somethin' hard comes into them. She almost spits out the word.

"Snake? Is that what you're tryin' to tell me? You run into a snake?"

"Uh, yes, ma'am, and I wouldn't be bringin' it up 'cept you axed me what happened. But I don't need to say no more about that snake. Is it that you're afraid of snakes, Big Maw? I'm sorry, uh, I didn't—"

She spits and growls. My tail starts to tuck.

"Let me tell you somethin' straight!" she screams. "This cat ain't afraid of no snake! This cat's quicker than a snake, doggone right she is—and there's a snake out there that knows that, too! Yes, he does. And one day I'm gonna meet that low-down, mud-suckin', belly-crawlin', baby-killin' coward again and he's gonna pay! Pay! Pay, do you hear me!"

She practically wails out the last part.

I've managed to get up on my feet. My doggy hair stands straight up on my back. I want to run for the pasture, but I think it's better if I just try to ease away—if she smacks me, I'll be one hurtin' dog. I'm rememberin' Blackie's tore-up ear.

Big Maw sees that I'm inchin' toward the door.

"Rascal, puppy," she says, her voice normal again, "I'm the one that's sorry. You couldn'a known why snake talk makes Maw crazy. I never told you my story. Now, c'mon, it's OK. You can tell Maw what happened."

I look up. Big Maw's eyes have got soft again.

"I shouldn't say any more, Big Maw. I'll just go over yonder behind some of that hay and get out of your way. I, uh—"

"No, I wanna know, puppy. I really do. You got waylaid by a snake, and I'm bettin' I know what snake it was. A big ole stumpy-headed cottonmouth, right?"

"Yes, ma'am."

"Was his name Ole Swamp?"

"He called hisself that. And big? Maw, he was fat as a melon in the middle. He opened his ugly ole mouth and showed me his fangs—like skinny long knives they were. I kept thinkin' he was gonna bite me and—"

"Shuh, puppy, a snake that wants to bite you will bite you long before you see him. That's how snakes are—cowards, every one of 'em. Sneakin' 'round, hidin' in the grass or in the hay or layin' low down under a log on the bayou bank. Waitin' and waitin'. A snake will wait all day and all night. Oh, they're somethin' when they get them stingers in you. They'll bite you and laugh in your face while that poison musses you up. They're brave then. But you get 'em out in the open or you catch 'em with their mouth or belly full and they ain't so brave. They'll run like rabbits from a marsh fire, I guarantee you that."

"Really, Big Maw? Ole Swamp didn't act like a snake that was 'fraid of nuttin'. He said snakes were the boss of the swamp and the woods and braver and smarter than any other critters. He didn't have one good thing to say about dogs—and nuttin' good 'bout cats, neither. And he seemed awful interested in my boy. I didn't like that. I, uh—"

A low growl rumbles from Big Maw's throat. Her eyes go slitty again. "Oh, he said all that, did he? Well, I can tell you for a fact that I know one thing he's afraid of—these."

She raises her right paw and flicks out her claws.

"One night I raked his tail good with these. The onliest problem is that I didn't rake him good enough and he got away."

This time my eyes get wide. "You got in a fight with Swamp? There ain't a dog in this yard that would tangle with Swamp, Big Maw. I—"

"A fight? I didn't get in no fight, Rascal. He come right in here in this very barn on the dark of the moon and bit one of my babies and was takin' him away—I caught him flat-bellied with that poor kitty mewlin' in his mouth. When I give him my wildcat wail, he dropped my baby and went sidewindin' for the door. I pounced and razored up his back good with my claws. Oh, he come back at me, thinkin' he was gonna get them stingers in me, too, but I swatted his ugly head silly. He's thinkin' nuttin's faster than a snake, but I give him one good enough to break his ugly neck."

Big Maw stops talkin'. She looks out far away and goes quiet for a while. Then she says, " 'Cept the real problem, Rascal, puppy, is that I didn't—I didn't break his fool neck. I was rearin' back to finish him off and send him back to the Devil he come from when I heard my baby moanin', all full of poison and callin' out for his momma. I run back, thinkin' maybe I could suck that venom outta my kitty, but he died in my paws. By that time, that snake had slithered out into the night. Like the coward that he is."

Big Maw stops talkin' and it gets real quiet.

I look at Big Maw. "Well, I'm sorry. That's a terrible story. I, uh . . ."

She looks at me and then looks down. In her eyes I see somethin' that I ain't seen before.

"Li'l Buster was his name. He was a strong li'l cat—a born rat biter. He was a handful and always into mischief, but I loved that li'l tom same as your momma loved you."

"Yes, ma'am. I'll bet you did. I'm real sorry. I didn't know."

"I know you're sorry, puppy. I know. I know you know what it feels like to lose somethin' you love. And I'm sorry, too. Oh, am I sorry."

Then somethin' hard comes back into Big Maw's eyes. "And I'll tell you what, Rascal. The thing that's really gonna be sorry one day is that snake. One day that snake is gonna be the sorriest critter that ever lived. I ain't done with him yet. Now, tell me, puppy, just what did that milky-mouth devil say to you? I just wanna know what kinda lies he was spreadin' 'round."

I'm so tired that I have to reach way back to try to 'member all the things Swamp said to me.

I tell her what he said about that dog King, and how he said King had attacked his snake lair way out in the woods and Ole Swamp only bit him in self-defense.

Big Maw throws her head back and laughs, but it ain't a funny laugh. "That scaly-headed, frog-suckin', mealy-mouthed, lyin' sack of crawfish dirt. I was *here*, Rascal, right outside this barn when it happened. That snake was on this farm, not out yonder in the woods in some stump. He was comin' for trouble. Lucky for the rest of us that ole dog sniffed him out. I didn't see the bite, but I heard King howlin', and I run out to see what the commotion was. I saw that poor ole dog runnin' with that snake still stuck to his nose—the Devil take me if I'm lyin'. He finally managed to shake that snake off, but by then it was too late. The way he died—that shouldn'a happened to a dog."

"I didn't believe that snake," I say, "but the way he talks, he could spin the moon around."

"Well, now you've learned somethin', Rascal. Never listen to a single thing a snake says. Not one."

"Yes, ma'am."

Things get quiet again.

After a while, I say, "Big Maw, would you mind if I curled up in that hay over yonder? I'm beat as Tante Lo-Lo's dust mop."

She nods. "You go on, Rascal. And if you ever need to come in Maw's barn like that again, just give a li'l bark. Maw will know it's you, and you won't have no problems. Now, you go right over there and find you a good, soft spot. Don't worry 'bout a thing. Ain't nuttin' gonna happen to you so long as Maw's around."

"Yes, ma'am. I 'preciate that. By the way, where are your boys?"

"They left early and went rattin' down by the bayou. I hope they get one. I ain't had a juicy rat in a coon's age. I got me a serious *envy* for a rat. You ever ate rat, Rascal?"

"No, ma'am, I ain't."

"You're missin' out."

"Really?"

"What's the best thing you ever ate?"

I have to think about this a second. "Well, I guess the store-bought food my boy gets me."

Big Maw smiles. "Store-bought food? Why, Rascal, ain't you got fancy! Now, listen, I ain't never had no store-bought food, but here's the thing. Think about the best bite of store-bought food you ever had, and rat tastes twenty-seven times better than that."

"Really?"

"Maw wouldn't jive you, puppy."

"What's rat taste like, Big Maw?"

She smiles this time and looks around, like somebody else could be listenin'. Then she whispers, "I ain't s'posed to know this, but rat tastes like chicken."

Then Maw has a big belly laugh.

I would laugh, too, 'cept I'm too tired.

I laze my way over to a pile of hay in the corner of the barn, thinkin' I might drop 'fore I get there.

I wonder if my boy is mad at me or worried 'bout me. What if he thinks I've run away from him?

He'd know better than that.

I get to the hay pile and slump down. And soon I'm way deep in doggy dreams.

I dream of woods that go on forever and a dark swamp at the edge and Momma somewhere sayin', "You watch out, Rascal. You watch out for yourself and your boy."

Chapter 5

Next thing I know, warm, hazy sunlight's pourin' through a high window in the barn and stabbin' at my blurry eyes. It's still a bit dim in here, but I know the light don't get up into that window 'less it's toward the end of the afternoon.

I've had me a pretty good dog nap.

I stand and stretch and yawn and try to shake the sleep from my head. My night chasin' bunnies and trompin' lost through the woods has left me stiff as them coon hides Nonc dries on the barn wall.

I'm hungry, but I'm not shore I'm gonna get any dinner.

I look around. Big Maw's layin' up on a bale of hay by the door, her chin restin' on her paws. She could be sleepin', but all dogs know that cats sleep with one eye open. Big Maw probly sleeps with both eyes open.

I trot quiet as I can toward the door. I get there and start to ease out when Maw says, "You had a good snooze, Rascal?"

"Yes, ma'am, I did, thank you. Did your boys get back?"

"Yes, they did, but no rats—never even saw one. They got them a mouthful of bird feathers is all. But they're learnin'. I'd tell you to go play with them but they're way up in the loft sleepin'. They wore themselves out."

"Yes, ma'am."

"You goin' to visit your dog friends?"

"I guess so. I'm wonderin' if my boy might have come to look for me. I figger the dogs would know."

Maw nods. "You like your boy, huh?"

"Yes, ma'am, I do. He seems to be the very best boy."

"Well, that's good, Rascal. I'm shore he is. With your momma gone, it's good that you got you a boy, and it's good that you got a good one. Some ain't so sweet as him, I can tell you that much."

"I've heard such. You ever had you a boy, Big Maw?"

Maw looks at me funny. "Haw, now that would be somethin', wouldn't it, Rascal? No, Maw's not the boy type. Ole Nonc Noon don't keep Maw around 'cause she's cuddly and cute. He keeps me around 'cause I do my job—I catch his rats and keep myself in babies so they can help me catch his rats. Otherwise, the rats in here would be thick as them fleas on ole Blackie out there in the yard. I was born wild and come here as a young girl from the garbage dump on the edge of town. I appreciate the setup I've got here—it beats the dump by an alligator mile. Now, you have a nice visit with them dogs, and if any one of 'em gives you guff, you just let Maw know, awright?"

"Yes, ma'am, I will."

I start to head out the door, then stop and look back at Big Maw.

"What if my boy hasn't come? What will I do then?"

Maw shakes her head. "Rascal, he's comin', but if for some reason he gets here after dark, you come right back here. No use you havin' to sleep out in the yard under that damp ole porch with all them fleabags."

Maw smiles at this. "Listen to me, Rascal. I guess I shouldn't be callin' your friends fleabags."

I smile back. I know she ain't said it bad. "Yes, ma'am, I'll come back if I need to, thank you."

I head on up the pasture toward the farmhouse, past them ole cows that just stare at me with their big cow eyes. I get to a spot, near Nonc's gate, where the dogs that sometimes ramble the pasture have dug a place to slip under the fence.

If I was home with my boy this time of the day, we'd be in his room. Most days he sits at a wood desk by the window and does what he calls homework. He grumbles about it a lot but says he's got to do it—Miz Henrietta wouldn't be happy if he didn't. He says she's been good to him and he cain't let her down.

I lay by his feet. He opens that window and there's usually a nice breeze blowin' in. Sometimes I just watch him or I snooze.

Sometimes he writes things in a book and then he reads them to me out loud. This is how I know all about his life before me. This is how I know he misses somebody.

He writes "Dear Momma" and such, though his momma's gone, same as my momma is. She didn't die chasin' a cane truck. She died havin' a baby and the baby died, too. It was long ago but he ain't forgot it. He was pretty much a puppy hisself when it happened.

Sometimes he writes "Dear Daddy." His daddy's gone, too, but he's not dead, though people think he is. But he's livin' like a stray down in a place called Florda for now 'cause some people had been chasin' after him—some people called the law.

Some people didn't like his daddy 'cause he's got the wild Injun in him—he's got mixed-up blood like most of the dogs on this farm. Which shouldn't matter to nobody, but to some people it does. Them law people told lies about my boy and his daddy, and his daddy had to run away. My boy says his daddy is smart and can live wild as a dog if he has to, so he's not too worried 'bout him gettin' caught, or findin' food and such. He just wishes things was different so they could be together. They used to have a fine ole time huntin' and fishin' and such.

Meely knows so much about the woods 'cause his daddy taught him good. They'd ramble everywhere together.

His daddy wrote him a letter not too long ago sayin' he was doin' OK in that place called Florda, mussin' with gators and such, and he would try to come sneakin' up one day to visit when things got better. Meely said nobody could know about that letter 'cept him, Miz Henrietta, and me. His daddy wrote that where he lives there's a beach where the sand looks like sugar and some water that's blue as the sky. He said Meely would have to come down sometime and see that.

My boy said he was gonna take the Greyhound one day and go. He said I was goin', too.

I'd like to ride on that Greyhound bus. That's the bus that brought my daddy to Nonc's place.

One day my boy hopes him and his daddy can live together again, but till then he's happy to be here 'cause nobody could be nicer to him than Miz Henrietta. He met her up at the schoolhouse—she was his teacher. He didn't always go to school reglar before he met her, but after he met her, he started goin' all the time.

When his daddy had to run off, Meely become a stray, too, so Miz Henrietta took him in 'cause otherwise they were gonna send him to the pound.

One time he wrote his momma a letter 'bout me. He writes her even though she's gone 'cause he says it makes him feel better, and, anyway, maybe she's listenin'. He says anybody who's looked up in the clear sky at night and seen the moon and all them stars knows there's things we'll never understand. For all he knows, she could be up there lookin' down at him. The letter said, "I got me a dog now, a great beagle pup named Rascal. He's *so* smart, Momma, that I almost think sometimes he understands every word I say."

I remembered that part 'cause it's true—I do understand just about everything he says.

I'm thinkin' 'bout my boy as I wander through the dog yard. I see them lanky ole deer hounds, Bon-Bon and Mamou, layin' up in a patch of sunlight in their pen. Mamou bothers to raise his head for a second and then puts it back down without so much as a woof. Bon-Bon don't even open her eyes. That's typical. Unless a deer run right through the yard or a bear come to chase 'em, them dogs cain't be bothered with nuttin' nor nobody.

The next dog I see is one that I don't particularly care to see—Blackie Grand Baton. Usually, he's got nuttin' good to say. He's lazin' next to the saggy cypress garage where Nonc parks his tractor and keeps a boat—what my boy calls a pirogue—that he uses to go paddlin' after frogs in the bayou.

Blackie's got his eyes closed, too, and I'm hopin' he's sleepin' but he ain't. He hears me and looks up.

"Hey, Rascal, what you doin' back 'round here? You miss the food? You miss your cat friends over in the barn?"

I nod at him but I don't say nuttin', since I don't know how to talk to grouchy dogs.

"Well, if it's the food you missed, you shoulda been here last night. Turnip stew with more cayenne than I got fleas—oh man. We mowed the lawn today, us dogs did."

I almost have to smile at this. Maybe Blackie ain't in a grouchy mood today, though I ain't gonna tell him I took a nap with Big Maw watchin' over me.

I'd never hear the end of it.

I figger I've gotta say somethin'—Momma would want me to be polite.

"I come back accidental," I say. I tell him some about my rambles last night but not about that snake. I don't want to talk about that snake no more.

"Homing instinct," says Blackie. "All dogs got it—even though this ain't your home no more. I was out runnin' deer in the great Atchafalaya one day—that was long, long ago, before I pitched up in this patch of paradise. I musta run twenty doggone miles chasin' a buck—chased that sonuvagun all the way to the next parish 'fore I pooped out. When I stopped, I had no more idea where I was than a flea knows whether he's on your head or your tail."

"What did you do?"

"I settled myself down on a li'l palmetto ridge and took me a rest. When I woke up, though it was pitch-black out and I was hungry enough to actually want to eat them turnips Tante give us last night, I had an idea of the way back. I just started walkin' a certain way, and when it didn't feel right, I would stop walkin' and close my eyes for a bit. And then I'd know again. Come right back to that double-wide where my Two-Footer lived at the edge of a sleepy ole bayou. It's a good thing to remember, pup, if you ever get lost out in them big woods again."

I nod.

"Of course, my Two-Footer didn't even seem to know I'd gone missin'. My water bowl was sittin' by the trailer steps dry as last summer's chicken bones. My food bowl was empty. I had to bark my fool head off just to get him to come outside and feed me. Stale rice from the icebox is all I got."

He shakes his head, disgusted.

I look Blackie over. He's near as big as them deer dogs but not near as handsome. Besides that raggedy ear that Big Maw chewed, he's got mangy black fur, with a splotch of gray and brown on his right rump, maybe from his Catahoula cur side. His ribs poke out. Half his tail ain't got no fur on it.

His face is long and pointy, and there's a skinny scar runnin' down his forehead and another zigzaggin' along his nose. The dogs say that's where them nootras bit him. One of his eyes is red and cloudy. The other one, though, is clear as mine, and I can tell there's some life in there.

I don't know what to say to this story. I don't know if

Nonc treats Blackie much better than that fella in the double-wide did.

Blackie keeps talkin'. He ain't said this much to me, ever.

"That's when I left and come over here. Took off that night. Every dog on the loose knows about Nonc. He ain't got no idea 'bout dogs, really, but for some reason he keeps takin' dogs in. Now, I didn't exactly get the red-carpet treatment like your daddy, Tubby, did. Nonc was 'bout to run me off 'cause I'm big and eat a lot and he already had them uppity ole hounds to chase them deers he never catches. But I had me a plan, see. I went over by them *roseau* brakes by the bayou and laid up there and waited for a nootra to come along. A big one did, just before dark, and I got him good and drug him up on the front porch and went to barkin'. Nonc come out cussin'—'Who's that loud dog barkin' on my porch!'—but when he saw that nootra-rat, he looked down at me and said, 'Well, looka you, big podnah. You might be good for somethin' after all.' So I knew I had me a job then. You know he gets a dollar a tail for them big ole rats? I make that man a lotta money, yes, I do. More than them deer dogs, that's for shore. They spend his money, considerin' all they eat and how they ain't never caught him a deer."

Blackie stops to flick at a fly that's landed on his nose.

He must see that I'm wonderin' about them nootras.

"Now, say, I don't s'pose you'd wanna team up, Rascal? All you'd have to do is be the tail biter—you're young and fast, so ain't no nootra ever gonna lay a tooth on you. I'd do all the hard work, breakin' their necks and all. And you know, it ain't just about makin' Nonc money. Them dog-gone nootras come from way down yonder beyond the gulf to invade our marsh, and they chewin' it up and spittin' it out like there ain't no tomorrow. They done run most of the poor muskrats out of their own land. It's a doggone shame what them nootras are up to."

It *does* seem a shame. But I ain't thought about chasin' no nootras.

Them big ones stink, and, anyway, they scare me with them big teeth they got—though I wouldn't admit that to Blackie.

"Well, my boy don't muss with nootras," I say. "He's a bunny boy and a squirrel boy, so I s'pose I should stick to huntin' what he hunts. But I 'preciate you axin' me."

Blackie nods. "I gotcha. But if you ever change your mind, you come see me, OK? I think we'd be a doggone good team, yes, I do."

"Well, thank you, Mr. Blackie. By the way, you ain't seen my boy, have you? I thought he mighta come lookin' for me."

"Cain't say I have. Ain't been nobody at all to bark at today 'cept for the mailman, and he don't come in the yard no more since a few of us got after his backsides one time."

"Y'all did?"

"Oh yeah. Tore a good ole hole in the bottom of his guv-ment khakis. Oh, he cussed us, and so did Nonc, though, 'tween us chickens, I don't think Nonc cares for that mail-man. He'll come up and wanna drink coffee half the mornin'. I think Nonc thinks he's a lazy so-and-so. And any-way, Rascal, we wadn't out to hurt the fella. Sometimes dogs just gotta have fun, you know what I mean?"

"Hhm-hhm," I say. "Well, it's been nice talkin' to you."

"You, too, Rascal. And watch out for them cats. They might claim to be nice to you now, but one day they'll turn on you like sour milk. That's what cats do."

I nod again. I know Big Maw is excitable, but I don't think she'd turn against me for no reason. But I know it ain't no use to argue with Blackie 'bout cats.

I trot on, with no real plan, and the next dog I see is Tubby LeBasset. He's up under the shade of a fig tree and gives me a friendly li'l bark. "Howdy-do, Rascal?" he says in his twangy voice. "Gosh durn, you're gettin' big. I thought you'd hightailed it out of here—got you a boy and were livin' on easy street. But I'm plumb tickled to see you."

I smile. "I'm doin' all right, though I do miss my friends." I tell him just what I told Blackie 'bout my big night out in the woods.

"Did you catch one of them ole rabbits?"

"No, sir, but I chased 'em good. I run into so many rabbits I didn't know which one to go after."

"Well, that's gotta be just a ton a fun. I get a hankerin' to go chase them bunnies now and then. But, well, ole Uncle's got me busy takin' care of all the gals around here, and that keeps me runnin' like a jackrabbit from a pack of wolves."

Tubby smiles when he says this. I smile back.

"Yes, sir. Sounds like a hard job, but somebody's gotta do it."

He laughs this time. "That's funny. You know, your momma used to say somethin' like that. She had some sense of humor, that gal did. I miss her like last night's T-bone."

"Yes, sir. Me too."

"'Tween us, Rascal, she was my favorite dog in the world. She was smart and sweet, and if a dog had troubles—and all dogs do sometimes—wadn't nobody better to talk to than Blanche. All the dogs on this farm felt that way. Even them deer dogs would come to see your momma."

"They did?"

"Oh, you bet your bottom dollar. Anyway, you know, don'tcha, that Bon-Bon, that bluetick gal, and your momma were distant cousins? You get your touch of bluetick from your momma's side of the family."

"Really? Momma never told me Bon-Bon was family."

"Well, you know how it is around here—the rest of the dogs think them deer hounds are snooty as a preacher's wife, and your momma didn't want anybody to think she was puttin' on airs by claimin' to be related to *them*. Now, if you want my opinion, I'm not so shore them dogs are stuck-up as much as they're just born solitary. They don't know how to keep any company other'n their own. Kinda sad, in a way. Now, us beagles—we *love* company, yes, we do. Ain't no dogs more sociable or sweeter than us beagles. Even them ticks bite us more than they do other dogs 'cause they think we taste like birthday cake."

I'm tryin' to take this all in. I knew I had bluetick in me, but I had no idea that Bon-Bon was a bluetick. If she was momma's cousin, she'd be my cousin, too. And if she's my relation, shouldn't we know each other?

Tubby keeps talkin'. "By the way, maybe you've heard— Bon-Bon is gonna have puppies. The daddy, ole Mamou, he's a redbone hound, so I been tryin' to figger out what them babies will be. Redticks? Bluebones? Tickbones? I think I'll start a contest, Rascal. You want in? The winner gets the next muskrat I drag in from the bayou. Haw-haw!"

My daddy, Tubby, is a character. He could talk a ham off a hog.

"That's funny," I say. "Sounds like you've already got the winners there."

"Well, your momma always said I had a way with words, Rascal. Yes, she did. So, you waitin' on your boy?"

"Yes, sir. I hope he's comin' soon."

"Oh, he's comin', Rascal. He knows what he's got."

"Yes, sir. I hope that's true."

I look around and realize the sun has ducked behind the sugarcane fields. The light's nice and soft, but that just means there's not much day left.

I shore wish my boy would hurry. I wanna sleep in my bed tonight or maybe even his.

I want supper.

Tubby yawns. "Well, good seein' you, hound doggy. I think I'm gonna take a li'l snooze, if you don't mind. Talkin' gets me tuckered out."

"No, sir. Go right ahead. I think I'll go up on the porch and give a bark or two. I think I'll let Nonc and Tante know I'm here. Maybe they'll tell my boy, if he don't already know."

"Good idea," says Tubby, yawnin'.

He closes his eyes. He's snoozin' 'fore I can walk away.

I trot up toward the broad porch, and a few other dogs—Tootie, Fuzzy, Poncho, Cisco, Belle, Beau, Sugarfoot, and Midnight—are layin' around the steps. They bark out hellos and how-ya-doin's. I bark back. They're all mixed-up dogs, with a bit of this and some of that, but they're nice dogs every one of 'em.

I like Sugarfoot best. She's a beauty—a small black dog, 'cept that she's got one white foot and a white splotchy patch over her right eye. She's got a cute black curly tail.

I feel kinda fidgety, though not in a bad way, every time I see her.

She comes up and gives me a sniff, and I sniff her back. She smells good. Sugarfoot's a bit older than me, not quite a puppy anymore.

"I don't s'pose you've come back to us, have you, Rascal? I've missed you since you got your boy."

"No, I got separated from my boy last night and ended up here, but he'll probly be here soon."

I wanna tell Sugarfoot I've missed her, too, but I don't. I'm bashful that way.

"How is it over there?" she says.

"It's good. He's the best possible boy—he's got a lotta dog in him, and it's a nice ole place, though not as big as this."

"Other dogs?"

"No, I'm the only dog. Lots of chickens, though."

"Them chickens tickle you, don't they?"

"I guess they do."

"Ain't it lonesome without other dogs?"

"It kinda is. But my boy makes up for it. We do a lot of dog things."

"Well, that's good, Rascal. And the lady?"

"She's nice as biscuits, though she don't have much dog in her. But I get plenty to eat. Store-bought food."

"Well, good for you. You ain't missed nothin' 'round here, really. It's the same ole dog's life—not that I'm complainin'."

I smile at this.

"You goin' up on the porch?"

"Yeah, I'm gonna bark at the ole folks to let 'em know I'm here. Maybe they know somethin' 'bout my boy."

"Good idea. I'll bark with you. Two barkers are better than one. The ole fella don't hear so good."

Me and Sugarfoot go up on the porch and start to barkin'. It takes a while, but I hear footsteps cloppin' toward the big green wooden front door to the house. Tante Lo-Lo opens it.

She's bony and skinny as a winter cow. She talks in a Cajun accent. Well, I guess I do, too.

"What y'all makin' that racket for, ehn? What's the matter wit' y'all dogs?"

I get up on my hind legs and bark again.

Tante puts her hands over her eyes and squints so she can see better.

"*Mais*, looka that—that doggone chicken-chasin' puppy's back."

She turns back. "Nonc, Nonc! Come yuh. That beagle you give Henrietta is back in our yard. Can you believe that?"

I hear Nonc hollerin' from deep in the house. "What? What's that you say? They got an eagle outside? An eagle in our yard? I ain't seen no eagles in a coon's age."

"Not an eagle, beb, a beagle! That li'l Rascal dog you give your niece for the boy she 'dopted."

"What? Some rascal's sneakin' 'round our yard? Should I get my 16 gauge, woman?"

Tante Lo-Lo shakes her head. She looks at us. "See what I gotta put up wit'?"

She leaves the door open but takes a couple of steps into the house. She cups her hands to her mouth and yells, "Beb, that beagle dog you give your niece come back to us. Come see for yourself!"

We hear more clompin' on the wooden floor, and soon Nonc shows hisself. He's tall and skinny, too, with a long red face and big ears. Such hair as he's got sticks out in tufts, like scraggly feathers.

"Huhn, well, looka that. I wonder if he run away from his boy?"

I bark—"No!"—but Nonc don't understand. He says, "Well, I better call Henrietta."

"Good idea," says Tante. "I don't want him chasin' my chickens, no. Every time he does, them hens go off and hide their eggs someplace I cain't find 'em."

I wanna tell her I'm done chasin' her chickens, but she wouldn't understand.

Nonc squints at me. He says, "Well, maybe we oughta catch him and tie him up on a rope till Henrietta and Meely can come get him."

"Good idea," says Tante.

I think this is a *bad* idea. My boy give me a collar, and I only wear it 'cause he wants me to. I don't like things 'round my neck.

Nonc stoops down and calls to me. He says, in a silly voice, holdin' out his hand, "C'mon, puppy dog. *Venez ici, mon cher petit chien.*"

I look at Sugarfoot, and she looks at me. "No way," I tell her. "I'm goin' back to the barn. If my boy comes, you bark at him and make him follow you there, OK?"

"OK, Rascal. I don't blame you. But ain't you afraid of that ole mean cat?"

I'm about to answer when Nonc reaches out and tries to grab my collar. I bolt, cat-quick, and go skitterin' off the porch in no time.

Nonc falls forward with a thud, and I hear him cussin'. I'm sorry for that, but I just won't be tied up.

I don't stop and look back till I'm clear to the pasture gate. I can see Nonc and Tante have come off the porch and are yellin' and wavin' their arms at me to come back. But I slip under that hole in the fence and go trottin' toward the barn, lookin' back every now and then to make sure they ain't chasin' me.

They ain't and I slow down. I get to the barn door and give a bark. After a while, Big Maw sticks her head out.

"Hey, Rascal. I guess your boy ain't come yet, huh?"

"No, ma'am. I barked ole Nonc out of the house, but he wanted to tie me up on a rope, so I run back here."

Big Maw nods. "I don't blame you, puppy. That ain't no way to treat a dog. Now, you come on in here. I'm shore Nonc's gonna call the lady now, so your boy should be here soon. Anyway, my boys, Boozoo and Doopsie, are here, and I'm about to tell them a story. You come on in and join us."

I trot over and settle in next to a hay bale. Big Maw's boys snuggle in next to her, and she starts to spin out a tale called "The Fat Rat and the Skinny Cat." It's a funny story, though maybe funnier to a cat than to a dog, and them rats probly wouldn't find it funny at all since they get ate in the end.

Maw puts on a funny voice when she tells it, in a kind of singsongy way.

I find myself noddin' off when there's a ruckus by the door and I hear voices. Maw stops talkin' and shushes the boys to be quiet, and I hop up, ready to run if it's Nonc come to put that rope on me.

The barn door pops open and there's lights shinin' at us, and then suddenly a light above the barn door comes on.

It's a dim ole light but not so dim that I cain't see my boy standin' there with his bulleye.

Nonc's there, too, but I don't care. I give a yelp and go runnin' toward my boy. He spots me and he comes runnin' toward me, too, yellin', "Rascal, Rascal, you crazy ole puppy, you, where you been!?"

And next thing I know I've jumped clean up into his arms and I'm lickin' his face and squealin' and he's nuzzlin' me like

crazy and sayin', "Oh, puppy, I'm sorry you got lost. I'm so sorry. It's all my fault."

Then he puts me down and stoops down with my face cupped in his hands and says, "You're some good dog. You made it all the way back here all by yourself. You're a tough puppy, and we just have to make shore we don't get separated again, OK?"

And I bark OK and give him another lick on the face.

Then he says sit, and I sit, and then he turns to Nonc, who's walked up behind him. For the first time, I notice the lady's with him, too.

"Thank you, Mr. Voclain, for callin' Miz Henrietta," says Meely. "We'd been runnin' all up and down the bayou lookin' for Rascal, and I know he was in good hands here. I 'preciate you lookin' after him."

I wanna say it was Big Maw who actually looked after me, but I 'preciate how my boy thinks about things.

"Aw, Meely, wadn't nuttin'," says Nonc. "I knew soon as I saw that dog you'd be worried sick. I tried to catch him so he wouldn't run off again, but he got away from me. But I had a feelin' he might be out here—for some reason, that puppy seems to like these ole barn cats."

I see Meely lookin' around, and in the dim light he spots Big Maw and her boys up on the haystack, just watchin' us.

Meely looks at me and says, "Stay, Rascal," holdin' up his hand like he does.

Then he starts walkin' over toward Maw and the boys.

"Be careful," says Nonc. "That ole momma cat's been known to take a chunk outta the hide of some of the big dogs in the yard. I don't know if she wants to be petted."

But Meely keeps goin', walkin' normal. He says, in a nice voice, "Well, look at you, ole momma. What a big ole beauty you are!"

Soon he's at the hay bale. Boozoo and Doopsie slip behind Maw, and I see Maw stiffen a bit, her eyes locked on my boy. But he eases right up to her and holds out his hand real slow so Maw can sniff it. Then he reaches over gentle and tousles her head.

I myself don't know what Maw might do, and I'm 'bout to bark at my boy to watch out. But then I see a funny thing.

Maw bows her big ole head and, just for a second, pushes it up against my boy's hand, her eyes closed. He rubs her soft behind her ears, and I could swear she's smilin'.

Then, just like that, Maw pulls away, stands, and jumps off the hay bale. Her boys follow her, and without a word they slip away slow to a dark part of the barn.

Meely comes back and kneels down beside me again and says, "Is that cat your friend, Rascal? Is that big ole cat your podnah?"

I give him a woof to let him know she is, and he laughs

hard at this. "Well, if that's the case, we'll have to come back and visit sometime. If it's OK with Mr. Voclain, of course."

Nonc nods. "Meely, you and Rascal can come yuh anytime, I mean it."

Meely stands and shakes Nonc's hand. "Thank you. And thank you again for lookin' after my pup."

Miz Henrietta speaks for the first time. "Yes, Nonc Noon. That phone call made our day. I really appreciate it. Now, we should be getting home, Meely. I believe there's still some homework to do."

My boy smiles. "Sorry to say, there is. C'mon, Rascal, let's go. You're so smart, you can help me figger my algebra."

"You wanna put him on a leash?" says Nonc.

"Naw," says Meely. "Rascal will stick close to me without one."

I give him a woof to that one, too.

Twenty bunnies runnin' over my back couldn't separate me from my boy tonight.

We head on up out of the pasture, my boy and Nonc shinin' the way with their lights. I follow Meely through the pasture gate, and as we pass the cypress garage where Tubby sleeps at night, I hear a voice whisper out at me from the dark.

Big Maw's slipped away from the barn to tell me goodbye.

"You take care, now, Rascal, and don't you be no stranger, OK? And by the way, your boy—he's all right. He ain't the worst boy that ever lived, no, he ain't."

I gotta smile at this. "No, ma'am, he's not. And I'm shore we'll be back sometime soon. You take care, too."

Chapter 6

I'm a real huntin' dog now, growin' bigger every day. My boy says I've got bluetick legs and bluetick feet.

Even that mean ole rooster in Miz Henrietta's yard don't bother me no more. Last time he come to chase me, I stood my ground and give him a good barkin' at. He circled me a few times, all puffed like he gets, and charged me. I hopped aside and got me a mouthful of tail feathers.

He run off cussin' me lower than a snake, but he ain't chased me no more.

Chickens is mean—maybe that's why people are always wringin' their necks.

Me and my boy are far in the woods behind Nonc Noon's farm. It's a day he calls Saturday, the first day of squirrel season. It's Injun summer, he says.

We got to the woods at first light. It was cool and foggy then, but it's got so warm that my boy's took off his long-sleeve shirt and tied it 'round his waist. His T-shirt has got wet spots on it from sweat.

There's a few skeeters buzzin' 'round, and my boy has put on what he calls bug dope. It stinks, which I guess it's s'posed to. Them skeeters fly in close thinkin' they've found break-fast, but then they buzz off.

We've caught four squirrels so far—them big ole red fox squirrels. My boy said that's all we need to catch today 'cause Miz Henrietta don't like to eat squirrels as much as he does. We're just ramblin' now.

The woods here are open, and it's easy walkin'. The trees are big and tall and there's lots of soft leaves on the ground, and lots of acorns, too, and plenty of spots where there's piles of acorns all cut up. My boy stops and says, "There musta been a reglar squirrel convention this mornin' up in these trees, Rascal. I've never seen a pile of cuttings this big. These squirrels we got ought to have some fat on 'em. There's lots of food in the woods this year."

We walk on for a bit, and the land starts to change till soon we're walkin' up against the bank of a small bayou—what my boy calls a slough. I look down into the water and see my reflection.

I guess I don't mind lookin' at myself. Meely says I'm a good-lookin' dog, and maybe I am. I don't look that long.

That water is clear and black, and it smells old. There's tiny minnows swimmin' 'round and water bugs, too. I'm thirsty, but this ain't water a dog would drink 'less he had to. And, anyway, my boy brings along a jug in his huntin' vest and gives me water out of that. It's sweet cistern water.

We keep walkin' and the ridge gets narrower and narrower till about all that's left is the levee, with the bayou on one side of us and a swamp pressin' close on the other. My boy calls out the trees he sees—hackberry and cypress and sweet gum and alder, moss hangin' from them everyplace.

Them cypresses go up and up and up. Some places, where the trees are far apart, you can see the blue sky through the treetops, and the sun stabs down like a giant bulleye shinin' on the black water.

The roots of them trees—what Meely calls cypress knees—poke up everywhere.

My boy stops and says, "Rascal, you ever see a place prettier than this? How 'bout we sit a bit?"

We just sit for a while, listenin' to the woods rustle all around us. Far off, we hear a crow cawin' and a woodpecker knockin' hard on a tree someplace. We see a hawk wheelin' high up in the sky in a break between the trees.

Somethin' goes flutterin' by quick, and my boy says, "Wood ducks, Rascal. Best-lookin' ducks you'll see anyplace in the world."

We sit like this for a good bit. I take a li'l doggy nap. I wake up when I hear a sound in the trees. I'm about to bark when my boy puts his hand up for quiet.

Soon, two big ole fox squirrels come skitterin' through the cypress tops and jump into a sweet gum tree just ahead of us. They go to feedin' on them gum balls. We just sit still and quiet and watch them go on by.

My boy stretches and swats at a skeeter buzzin' 'round his face, then says, "OK, pup, let's get goin'. There's an ole bridge over a sleepy bayou up ahead that connects this ridge to a big oak ridge on the other side. I ain't never crossed it, though Daddy and I come up to it one night bulleyein' for coons. We were tuckered out by then, but Daddy had gone over there by himself once and said it's one of the sweetest stretches of timber he ever saw. I think we should go take a look."

Anyplace my boy wants to go is fine with me, so we head on out.

We go slow as usual. The narrow bayou we're followin' twists and turns every which way. We come 'round a bend, and the levee rises up a little. The trees have thinned out here, and the sun is shinin' down on a grassy patch just ahead of us. The walkin' gets a bit harder—there's palmettos and some twisty vines and roots runnin' along the ground.

My boy points off toward a small hill risin' up out of the swamp. Scrubby trees and palmettos are coverin' the top of it.

"See that place there, Rascal? Daddy says that's an Injun burial mound—Injuns used to roam this country long, long ago, before folks like us ever got here. I've got some Injun in me from Daddy's side, though Daddy says our Injun relations lived way, way down in the salt marsh near the Gulf of Mexico, a far piece from here. Daddy says this is sacred ground and we should always move by such a place slow and respectful and never muss with it."

We stand quiet for a while, then we head on out again.

We walk on and find another place where the levee rises up again even higher than the last spot. Suddenly I smell somethin' I don't like—don't like at all.

A growl jumps out of me.

My boy already sees what I smell.

"Whoa, Rascal, whoa. Stay back, boy! You stay, OK?"

I don't see no snake, but I smell him good. I don't want him nowhere near my boy. I start barkin' my head off.

My boy's already got a bead on him.

"It's OK, Rascal—just settle down. And stay. I'll take care of this bad boy. Look at this thing—he's a beauty."

I'm wonderin' if my boy's gonna catch that snake like he does them squirrels. But he puts his gun down, across a log close by, and looks around. He sees a scrubby tree on the bayou edge. He takes a knife out of his pocket and quick cuts off a limb 'bout as big around as his thumb and shaves off some small branches so that there's a fork at the end of it.

He looks back at me and says, "Now, you stay—I mean it. This is a baby copperhead, not two foot long. A big snake, unless you corner him or step on him, won't waste his venom—he'll usually run. But some of these li'l fellas can be full of fight and bite. I don't want him bitin' you, OK?"

I don't like anything my boy's said. He don't know that I know all about snakes from meetin' Ole Swamp.

I start to bark again, tryin' to tell my boy to not muss with that snake.

He grins and bends down, givin' me a nuzzle. "It's OK, puppy, really. I've handled much bigger snakes than this. It's another thing Daddy showed me. I'll be fine. I just wanna check this fella out."

I go to whimperin', but when he stands, I shush and hold still like he's told me to.

I'm shiverin' all over. I'm worried.

My boy looks forward, and I look, too, hopin' that snake's crawled off. But he ain't. He's coiled up in a sunny patch, his wedgy head pokin' up just above the grass tops.

Meely moves ahead with his forked stick, talkin' to that snake.

"Well, whatta we got here, ole son? Look at you. You're somethin' else."

That snake sees Meely now and rises up, his tongue dartin' every which way.

"Look at your color," my boy says. "You're just a beautiful beast."

He reaches out with that stick, and that snake strikes the end of it—*whack!*

Meely laughs. "Feisty, ain't ya?"

Instead of movin' back, my boy moves toward the snake and prods him with the forked end of his stick. This confuses that snake—I guess he ain't use to somethin' comin' back at him.

He rears up to strike again, but my boy is cat-quick, pokin' that snake just under his chin with that fork end. This confuses that snake even more, and he turns and starts to slither away.

I'm hopin' my boy will just let him go, but he don't. He takes two quick steps and jabs down with his stick. I cain't see what's happenin'. Another bark just jumps outta me.

My boy bends down, reachin' with his right hand. I start barkin' like mad now. "No, Meely, no!"

Too late. He comes up holdin' that snake right behind his head. It ain't happy. It's wrigglin' good, but my boy grabs it by the tail with his free hand and talks soft to it.

That snake settles down.

"Looka this creature, Rascal. I've never seen a copperhead so bright this late in the season."

I get the *frissons*. My ears go flat.

"It's OK, puppy. I got him good. Come over and take a good look. Get a good sniff. If you see any snake like this, you just stay away. They ain't bad critters, really—but you don't want to get bit by one."

I'm not goin' over to my boy. I just cain't. He don't know that I already know more 'bout snakes than I care to.

He walks toward me and kneels down, though not too close. "This might be the best-lookin' snake out here. He's just a highland cottonmouth, really—first cousin to the water moccasin. The grown-ups will get to be four or five foot. A lot of people just shoot these critters soon as they see 'em, but Daddy never would unless a snake threatened to bite him. He says it ain't right. He says all creatures got their place in the woods. They're all tryin' to make a livin' just like we are."

My boy must not have heard the story about that poor dog King; otherwise, he wouldn't be talkin' nice about snakes.

For the first time, that nasty li'l crawler sees me.

"What you lookin' at?" he says, all smart-alecky.

"Well, not your ugly self."

"You wouldn't be sayin' that if I was free."

"Oh yeah? Well, you wouldn't be sayin' a word if my boy was like a lot of other boys."

"I ain't afraid of no boys or Two-Footers of no kind. Not none. Not even the ones with them boom sticks."

"Well, then that just makes you the dumbest snake that ever crawled. And, anyway, I saw you startin' to run."

"I wadn't *runnin'*, you dumb, pitiful dog. I was crawlin' away slow and only after I got tired of his li'l stick game."

"Game? Tired? Ha! You tried to bite my boy, and he juked you out with that stick and then pinned your pointy head to the ground when you tried to get away. I saw you slitherin' off."

"Oh, you mean like a whupped dog runnin' from a fight? That might be you, but that ain't me. Anyway, what you doin' insultin' me? I ain't the one picked the fight."

I snort at this. "Ain't nobody fightin', and, anyway, you saw us comin'—or you shore heard us or smelt us. You shoulda just crawled away. A smart snake woulda done that."

He hisses back. "Oh, I see. I'm out here mindin' my business, and you and your Two-Footer come bargin' through *my* territory and *I'm* the one that's s'posed to get out of the way? I don't think so. You dogs got you some strange notions."

One thing I've learned about snakes. They could talk a flea off a dog.

I don't know what to say to that.

"Cat got your tongue?" he says. "Haw-haw."

He sounds just like Ole Swamp.

"No, but I know a cat that could get yours."

"As if."

"Well, come over to Voclain's Farm and I'll introduce you to Big Maw. She's ate bigger snakes than you."

He hisses at this. "Ain't no cat never gonna eat a snake."

"Well, not one as ugly as you."

He looks at me hard, then laughs.

"Well, that ain't what your boy says."

"Whatta you mean?"

"You heard him. He says I'm a beauty. He says us copperheads are the best-lookin' snakes out here."

"He don't mean it that way. He thinks *everything* is beautiful. Even them creepy ole spiders."

"You're jealous, ain't you, dog?"

"Of what? A snake? Never!"

He actually smiles. "I don't believe that. Your Two-Footer thinks I'm a beautiful beast. I'll bet he ain't said that about you."

"He *has!*"

"Has not."

"Has. He thinks I'm the best dog God ever let live."

"Well, that shore cain't be true."

Some people say it don't do no good arguin' with a mule. I've now added snakes to that list.

Still, I'm 'bout to say somethin' back when my boy lifts that snake up a bit higher to get a better look at him. Then he says, "All right, ole son. It's time for you to go."

He stands and walks a few steps and puts that copperhead gentle on the ground, headfirst. He lets go of the head but is still holdin' on to the tail, keepin' it up high so that snake cain't wheel around on him. But that snake knows he's 'bout to get sprung 'cause he just lays there. Meely lets go his tail and stays real still. The smart aleck don't hang around. Soon as he knows he's free, he skeedaddles off into the grass and disappears.

Good riddance, I say.

Meely comes over to me, bends down, and gives me a pat on the head.

"OK, Rascal. Keep an eye peeled. Sometimes when you see one copperhead you'll see a bunch of 'em."

This ain't what I want to hear.

We go on, my boy tuckin' his gun in the crook of his left arm, barrel down, and usin' his snake stick as a walkin' stick, sometimes beatin' the tall grass ahead of us to make shore there ain't no snakes layin' up waitin'. I've got my nose up, sniffin' every which way, just in case.

We walk on, the levee curvin' in a big bend, to a spot where the cypresses press up hard and thick against both sides of the levee. There ain't much sun gets in here, which makes the walkin' easier 'cause it keeps the brush down.

That's good. I already know snakes don't like the shade as much as they like the sun.

Soon, we come to that bridge my boy talked about.

It don't look like much to me—narrow and made of wood. The railin' on one side has busted clean off. I see part of it down in the bayou below. I trot ahead, sniffin'.

I smell rot and damp.

Some small cypresses and other crooked ole trees are pokin' up out of the slough on both sides of the bridge.

Meely comes up behind me to look it over, too.

"This bridge has seen better days, ain't it, Rascal? Daddy told me that farm tractors used to cross over this bayou on the way to some hayfields a fella had planted on part of the big ridge on the other side. But ain't no tractor been back here in a coon's age—I'd say no people, either, from the looks of it."

We stand like this for a long time, my boy lookin' around. Then he says, "Well, whattaya say, puppy? You wanna go explorin'?"

Actually, I don't. I don't like the smell or look of things. I try to tell my boy this by turnin' around and startin' to trot back.

I hear him laugh. "What, have I tired you out? C'mon, Rascal. Let's have us an adventure and see what's on the other side. C'mon, puppy."

He turns to go, droppin' that walkin' stick and shiftin' his gun to his right hand. He starts to walk across that rickety bridge, stickin' to the planks on one side since there's holes in the other. When he gets about halfway across, he turns to me. I ain't moved. I just don't wanna go over there. I've got a bad feelin', the way dogs sometimes get a bad feelin' about things.

"Rascal! Whatcha doin', pup? C'mon, you cain't let me go have this adventure by myself, and I shore ain't gonna leave you here."

He then gives a whistle and starts to walk backwards— when I hear a sharp crack.

Suddenly I see my boy tumblin' over backwards, his gun flyin' out of his hand.

It goes clatterin' on the planks behind him.

He cries out—cries out like a dog stung by birdshot.

He yells, "Oh God, Rascal! Oh no!"

Chapter 7

I bolt for my boy, rickety bridge or not.

He's sprawled on his back, eyes closed. He's moanin' loud.

I'm lookin' to see what's happened and realize that one of his legs has broken clean through the planks.

I sniff.

I smell blood.

Tears are runnin' down his cheeks. I give him a lick—I bark to tell him it's gonna be all right.

He opens his eyes.

"Doggone, Rascal. Oh, puppy, I just did the stupidest

thing in my life. Oh Lord, what an idgit I am. No wonder you didn't wanna cross this bridge. Them planks are soft as white bread."

My boy ain't an idgit. If I'da come when he called me, maybe he wouldn'a been walkin' backwards like that. He'da seen them rotten spots.

This is all my fault.

I whimper, though I don't want to. It just comes out. I lick him again 'cause I cain't think of what else to do.

I feel his warm hands on me, rubbin' my ears. He pulls me close.

"That's nice," he whispers. "I 'preciate them kisses. Now, lemme see if I can get myself outta here. Gimme some room here."

I back off and Meely uses his hands to push hisself up to a sittin' position. He comes up slow. He makes a face I ain't seen before.

"Oh, Rascal, I'm hurtin'. I feel like I've got a snappin' turtle latched onto my lower leg. I cain't seem to even move it. It's stuck. Somethin's got me caught."

He looks down at his leg. There's blood oozin' from his jeans where his leg is jammed through the planks.

"Oh man, I've messed up big-time, ain't I?"

I don't know what to do. I come up and lick him again. I start to whimper. I bark and bark and bark.

He nuzzles me. "It's OK. It's OK. Lemme just think about this for a minute. Somethin's got me pinned down there, and I don't know what it is."

My boy closes his eyes again and goes quiet. Then he opens them and looks down at his stuck leg. He presses 'round the part where there's blood and says, "Ouch, that's tender." He then starts to poke his fingers down around the hole his leg fell into. In some places, the wood just crumbles, crumbles enough so that he can look down to where his leg is danglin'.

"Well, Rascal, this ain't good. Either a spike or a big ole splinter has got me caught. I'm not shore I can reach down there far enough to pull it out. And even if I pull it out, I could go to bleedin' bad."

He stops talkin' and looks around. "Hmm, puppy. Would you remind me to listen to you next time? Now I know why you didn't wanna cross this stupid ole bridge."

He tousles my head and then leans forward and gives me a long hug. We go quiet for a while.

Finally, Meely speaks.

"Rascal, here's the deal. You gotta go get some help. I'm stuck to this bridge like syrup on a cold day. Can you find your way to Nonc Noon's farm? Can you go get Nonc and have him follow you back here? I know you're the smartest dog on earth, so I need you to do that for me. Otherwise, I'm afraid I'm in deep, deep trouble."

I know what my boy is sayin', but I know one other thing: I ain't leavin' him here all by hisself, what with copperheads slitherin' 'round and who knows what other critters creepin' about.

I need to stay here and guard him like a dog does.

That's a dog's job.

I start barkin', tryin' to bark that out.

But it's as if he's read my mind.

"Pup, you cain't stay. It could be dark before Miz Henrietta gets worried enough to send anybody to look for us. And no-body knows that we've gone this deep into the woods. I might not last all night. You gotta go—I'm countin' on you. Go fast as you can, and let's hope ole Nonc is wearin' his hearin' aid."

I still don't wanna go, but I know what my boy's sayin' is true. Only thing is, I'm not shore I can find my way all the way to Nonc's.

What if I get lost?

Another whimper crawls out, and I start to shake all over.

Meely pats me again. He says soft, "Now don'tcha be worried, Rascal. You're some dog, and 'member, you got that bluetick in you. You can do anything you put your doggy mind to. Now, you go on. Go."

He points back across the bridge.

"Go on, now," he says gentle. "Get me some help."

I give my boy one more lick and then look around. There's one thing I've got to do before I go.

I back up and wriggle my way 'round my boy. He tries to grab on and stop me, but I slip away.

"Whoa, pup, whatcha doin'? You're goin' the wrong way, Rascal. C'mon, you need to get goin' quick. No foolin' around."

My boy sounds cross, but I know what I'm doin' is right.

He turns his head to look at me.

I scamper over to his gun, which has landed in a place where he cain't reach it. I get my teeth around the barrel and start tryin' to drag it to him.

That barrel tastes bitter—oily and such—and it's hard for me to keep a grip on it 'cause it's slippery. But I'll feel better if my boy has his shooter.

If them nasty ole snakes come crawlin' 'round, they'll be sorry.

I hear him tryin' to laugh as I keep tryin' to drag it to him, though he's hurtin' too much to laugh for real. The gun keeps slippin' outta my mouth, and that oily taste is startin' to gag me.

I growl at the gun a few times and finally drag it close enough so that he can reach back and grab the barrel hisself.

He pulls it up close to him and rests it across his lap.

I give him a bark. I stand up on my hind legs and jump up and down.

He tries to laugh again through the hurtin'.

"Oh, what a smart, smart, smart dog you are. I'm sorry I sounded cross. Now, I've got this gun and I'll be fine. You go on, puppy. Go fetch Nonc Noon."

I stand for another coupla seconds, lookin' at my boy. I *still* hate to go. So I bark twice to tell my boy to watch out, and then I turn and race around him off that bridge, runnin' as hard as I can run.

It's already the middle of the afternoon, and I know what my boy has said about gettin' caught in the dark is true. It'll be bad for him if he does. If a snake don't get him, them skeeters could come and just carry him away.

I hit that open part of the levee and go scrabblin' along like a deer runnin' from a whole pack of bluetick hounds, but I don't get too far when somethin'—a vine or root or somethin'—trips me up.

I tumble forward, rollin' head over heels a couple of times, bouncin' in the soft dirt and leaves, mad at myself for not watchin' out better.

But when I've stopped rollin' and start to pick myself up, two things smack me hard as Tante Lo-Lo's broomstick handle.

One is the stink of a snake in the air.

The other is a voice sayin', "Hold on, puppy. Not so fast. You'll burn yourself out quick runnin' like this. You need to get this right—'cause your boy's in more trouble than you could possibly know."

Chapter 8

I come up growlin' fierce as somethin' slithers past me.

Ole Swamp has reared his ugly self up a few feet ahead. He's in my path, and there ain't no way past him on this narrow levee.

I bark loud, my hackles risin'. "Don't you come near me, Swamp. You might bite me, but I'll chew you in two before that poison gets to me. Back off and let me get outta here. My boy's been hurt, and you're just in the way."

"Whoa, whoa. Hold on, Rascal. You got it all wrong, son. I tripped you up to slow you down. I know your boy's hurt—I saw it happen. You got a long way to go to fetch ole Uncle. You need to pace yourself and make shore you get there—make shore you don't get your fool self lost."

"You're lyin'!" I bawl. "You don't care whether I burn out or get lost or not. You just wanna hurt my boy—you—"

"Rascal, how many times I gotta tell you—if I wanted to hurt you or your boy, I already woulda done it. Soon as you trot off, I'm gonna go over there just outta sight of him and stand guard. I'll watch him till you get back."

I growl at this. "You better not go nowhere near my boy! He might be stuck and he might be hurt, but he's got his gun and he'll turn you into snake mush the minute he sees you. I got that gun for him 'cause I knew creepy ole snakes like you might be crawlin' 'round tryin' to do somethin' bad."

I hear a low hiss. "Dog, calm down. I know he's got that boom stick. I saw what you did, and, fine, you're a certified doggy hero. Ain't you special? But see, even if I go over there, he *won't* turn me into snake mush just 'cause he's got that gun. Unless I go chargin' at him, he'll just sit there nice and quiet and watch me 'cause, like you know, your boy thinks us snakes are OK. You know I'm talkin' the truth."

I shake *my* head. "No snake talks the truth."

"Well, believe what you want, but I been followin' y'all for a while. I saw how he handled that li'l copperhead y'all come across earlier. Now, I don't think Two-Footers oughta be fondlin' snakes for fun out here in *our* woods. But no harm done, and he called that li'l snake a *beauty*. I heard it myself. So did you."

I look at Swamp. "You're a lyin' sack of scales. Why were you *followin'* us in the first place? You already told me you ain't got no use for Two-Footers, or dogs, neither. Why would you be creepin' 'round behind us 'less you're up to no good?"

Swamp cocks his head at an angle. "Now, you're a hard case, ain't you, puppy? OK, here's the deal. I was followin' you to *protect* you."

I snort at this. "Protect us? From *what*?!"

At this, Swamp swivels his head around, his tongue tastin' the air, as though he's lookin' for somethin' or smellin' for somethin'.

Then he comes slitherin' my way.

I growl and find myself startin' to back up, but he's up on me before I know it.

"Rascal," he says all whispery. "You think I'm a big, bad snake? Well, son, you don't know what a big, bad snake looks like. See, it's kinda complicated, but I got a cousin

94

named Pick. You know why he's called Pick? 'Cause it's short for Ice Pick. He ain't got but one fang—but that's how long and sharp it is—the size of a ice pick. Lemme ask you somethin'. How long do you think I am?"

"I dunno and I don't care."

"Better than six foot and proud of every smooth-crawlin' inch. But Pick—he's nine and a half foot long. You listenin' to what I'm sayin'? We're talkin' 'bout a monster. A hide hard as nails. He can swallow a grown duck or a whole chicken. He once killed and ate a three-foot alligator. He's hungry all the time. He kills for *fun*. Some snakes say he eats his own young and any snake that crosses him is dead—in fact, there are some snakes who say Pick is invincible, that he's got some kind of snake mojo, that he *cain't* be killed."

Swamp stops to let this sink in.

"And, Rascal, what Pick hates most is them Two-Footers and any critters that run with them. He *invades* farmyards, lookin' for a fight."

"So?" I say. "I don't care about a big, dumb, mean snake named Pick. I just need to get goin' to get help for my boy. Now just move aside."

Swamp shakes his head again. "Rascal, what I'm tryin' to tell you is that Pick's on your boy's trail. It's *him* he's after. I was tastin' the air and picked up a faint scent a good ways back. It was Pick or I'm a purple turtle. He's the muskiest crawler out here. Now, he could be on *my* trail as well. He probly wants a piece of me worse than he wants a piece of your boy. And you."

I look at Swamp hard, tryin' to read him. I don't want to believe him, but somethin' suddenly stirs in me.

I look past him, sniffin' the air. I catch a scent—
somethin' on the breeze comin' from behind Swamp. It's
faint, but a *frisson* crawls down my back.

"OK," I say. "Why would Pick be after us? We ain't never
done nuttin' to him. Never crossed his path."

"It don't matter," says Swamp. "He hates all Two-
Footers. He wants a war—he wants them farmers to come
after him. He *wants* to bite and kill a Two-Footer. Don't you
understand that? And that ain't the half of it. He'll crawl up
into farmyards, even go for kittens and puppies, right in
front of their mommas and daddies. He'll—"

"Oh, and what about you?" I growl. "You're just a
sidewindin' liar. You lied to me about that dog, King. You
killed him right there in Nonc's pasture. Big Maw told me
she saw that poor dog die right there in the barnyard. And
you killed her kitten—snuck in durin' the dark of the moon
and bit her baby. She got her claws into you before you slithered off like a coward in the dark. You're makin' this up so
you can go hurt my boy!"

Swamp ain't lookin' at me no more.

"Cat got *your* tongue?" I say. "Now, move aside, Swamp.
I mean it. I'm comin' through."

The last part comes out in a growl.

"OK, Rascal, I know what it seems like. But I'm sorry to
report that none of that is true."

"It *is* true."

"No, it ain't."

"Is, too! And you're here wastin' my time—you're—"

"Rascal, listen close. OK, a snake did bite King in the
barnyard, and a snake did kill that kitty—but it wadn't me."

"Liar! You *told* me you bit King. You *confessed!*"

Swamp puts his head down like he's thinkin'. "OK, I know what I said, but I was just tellin' tales. It ain't a bad thing for a snake to have Two-Footers and their dogs be afraid of him—to think he's the worst, most dangerous snake that ever lived."

"Just what *are* you sayin', Swamp? If you didn't bite King or kill Maw's baby, who did?"

"Rascal, I thought you were a smart dog, 'stedda one of them slow-footed flea brains. Who do you think did it?"

"Pick?"

"Good guess, puppy. Pick done it, not me."

I shake my head. "I still think you're lyin'. I still think you're tryin' to confuse me. I think you're—"

Swamp looks around again, then says, "OK, hold up. If I killed that cat's baby, then I ought to be wearin' proof of it on my back, right? You said yourself the cat got her claws into that snake good. If that's true, then where's my scars? C'mon—come take a good look. You see a scar on me?"

Swamp swivels hisself around, and—it's true. He ain't got a mark on him.

"See."

This makes my head hurt.

"OK. Maybe that's true. But I still don't understand why you want to *guard* my boy. If Pick comes 'round and musses with him, he'll get to suck a mouthful of squirrel shot. My boy don't need you."

Swamp lets out another low hiss. "Rascal, Rascal, I'm disappointed in you. Here I've showed you my deepest snake heart and you still think I'm the Devil. OK, I'll try one more time. I want to guard your boy 'cause, well, 'cause, 'cause . . ."

He stops, like it's just somethin' he cain't say.

" 'Cause why?"

He looks at me with his cocked head again, then slithers ever closer and says in a whispery voice, "It kills me to admit this—just kills me. But your boy saved my life."

Chapter 9

"What!?" I bark. "What? You're lyin'! You're crazy! You're—"

"OK, simmer down. I'll make this quick as possible 'cause you gotta get yourself goin'. See, I was out here in this very neck of the woods one day and run into a li'l problem. Pick had come after me 'cause he hates me as much as he hates Two-Footers and dogs. I'm against him startin' a war we cain't win. I've talked a lot of snakes over to my side. Pick just *hates* that. After we boxed for a bit, I could tell the big, ugly lug was gonna take me in that kind of fight, so I ran. I ain't afraid of Pick. I ran so I could fight another day. But in runnin', I made a big mistake—I ran into a whole pile of boys."

Swamp stops to lift his head again and taste the air with his tongue. Then he goes on. "Anyway, they were noisy, crazy boys with guns and sticks. They caught me out in the open. I knew my only chance was to try to spook 'em, so I kept rearin' up and givin' 'em a lot of fang and hissin'. They kept tryin' to whack me with them sticks, but I got 'em jumpy as frogs, so they missed every time. Then, the biggest of the galoots—a fella they kept callin' Junior—says, 'Back off, idgits! We'll pepper him with birdshot at the same time. We'll blow his guts all over the woods.' "

Swamp stops talkin' to let this soak in.

"So that was it—Ole Swamp here was about to become buzzard food when I hear some other boy yellin', 'Hold on. That's *my* snake! I want that snake!' Well, I'm kinda surprised 'cause I ain't nobody's snake, but I guess them wild boys were surprised, too, 'cause they shut up and stopped swattin' at me. Then this boy comes from out of nowhere, and he says, 'Do you podnahs mind if I take this snake alive? Me and my daddy c'lecks 'em. They're worth good money that way.' This stumps the wild boys for a bit till one of them says, 'You're crazy. No way you gonna take that snake alive. He'll bite you and you'll drop dead on the spot.' And this boy says, 'Anybody wanna bet? I got a quarter in my pocket says I get him.' And then that Junior fella says, 'Hah, a quarter ain't worth nuttin'. I say we just kill this snake and get it over with.' But this boy says, 'Aw, c'mon, Junior. Lemme have some fun. Lemme just catch this snake and then you can have him.' "

Swamp looks at me. "You followin' this, Rascal? So then the one they call Junior says, 'Fine. You wanna get your sorry butt bit, it ain't nuttin' to us. We'll let you swell up and die out here in the woods.' That boy just laughs. He says, 'Stand aside.'

"Now, me, I'm of a mind to run, but I know the wild boys will shoot me if I do. So I've got to take my chances with this fool. For all I know, he's gonna catch me by knockin' me in the head. I see he's got a stick in his hand. But he comes up and looks at me funny and says some mumbo jumbo—and then he winks at me. Winks at me like I might understand. I coil up and give him a good hiss. I show him the white of my mouth 'cause I don't want them other fools to think we're in cahoots. But he turns out to be bird-quick with that stick, and he pins my head and grabs me good and hard—but not so hard that he's hurtin' me. I feel like I have to put up some sort of a fight, but I don't put up much. And he holds me up, and I'm taller than him—my tail is draggin' on the ground, I'm not lyin'.

Then he says to them wild boys, 'Too bad you didn't bet those quarters. I'd have a dollar fifty now.'

"I'm watchin' those wild boys, and all of them—save for Junior—could catch blackbirds in their mouths. But Junior says, 'Well, ain't you special. Now, throw that snake down so we can shoot it proper. Give it over like you said you would.'

"The boy don't answer. Instead, he turns his back on them and looks up at the sky and speaks some more gibberish. Then he whispers, 'OK, ole fella, let's run these fools off.' He turns

and looks at Junior and says, 'I just had a talk with this snake, and his grandma knew my grandma, and it wouldn't be polite to hurt a friend of the family. He really ain't a bad snake, and I'd like you to get to know him better.'

"Then he tosses me—I'm serious—at that big fool."

Swamp stops again, like he expects me to say somethin'.

I could catch a blackbird in my mouth, too.

"So there I am, tumblin' head over heels, and next I know there's screamin', and next I know I'm thumpin' hard into Junior, but not as hard as I might 'cause Junior has pitched hisself backwards, tryin' to get outta the way. I thump into Junior and then I hit the ground, and, well, I'm a bit dizzy 'cause snakes ain't used to flyin'. And I see Junior on the ground backin' away on his hands as fast as a Two-Footer can. He don't have his boom stick no more—he'd flung it away when he fell. Meanwhile, them other boys have run off hollerin' and crashin' through the brush like cows from a swampcat. Then the boy rushes up and gets between me and Junior and says, 'If I were you, Junior, I wouldn't hang around. I can tell when snakes are riled up, and this one is plenty riled up. You better get out of these woods.'

"Junior picks hisself up and says, 'You're crazy, you know that? I'm gonna get you for this one day.' And I hear that boy sayin', 'Oh yeah? Well, I'll just get outta the way and let you and this snake work it out.' He steps aside so it's just me and Junior eye to eye. I open my mouth wide and cock my fangs and rear back, and, well, the scream that comes out of Junior's mouth even scares the frogs out of me. He lights out fast as a duck leaves the water and goes crashin' through the woods stumblin' and cussin' all the way. He don't even stop to grab his gun."

Swamp stops and swivels his head around again, tongue flickin' the air, like he's listenin' for somethin'. Then he turns back to me.

"So that was your boy. After that Junior character run off, he told me to skeedaddle and I did. Now, I'm not sayin' I liked bein' pinned down like that, and I'm not sayin' I 'preciate him throwin' me around that way, either. But it's way better than what them wild boys woulda done to me."

Swamp stops again and gives me a look I ain't seen before. "So, here's the deal. He saved my skin, so I'm gonna hang around and watch him till you get back. Then we're even and all bets are off. Now, you get outta here and don't burn yourself out, Rascal, OK? Remember, you've got to come all the way back out here."

If Swamp is lyin', it's some lie.

"OK," I say. "I'm goin'. But, Swamp, listen to me. If you're tellin' tales and you hurt my boy or even *try* to hurt my boy, I'm gonna run these woods till I track you down, I don't care how long it takes, and I'm gonna break your snake neck. I swear by the bluetick hound in me I will."

Swamp actually nods at this. "Puppy," he says, "you're gettin' a bit melodramatic. I'm a snake of my word, and if I break my word, then I'll deserve to have my neck broken. Now, just get goin'. And, oh, watch for Pick. You'll smell him before you see him. He's big and slow and stupid, but whatever you do, don't let him corner you. He'll hypnotize you with them snake eyes, and they'll be the last things you'll ever see.

"I mean it, Rascal. If you get cornered, well—have fun in doggy heaven."

Chapter 10

I light out, tryin' not to go too fast or too slow or to think how far it might be to Nonc Noon's farm. I'm tryin' not to think about Pick.

The first part is easy—I just gotta follow this levee till it plays out. Then I'll hit the wide woods and hope I can pick up the scent we left comin' in and follow it back. Otherwise, I'll just have to figger it out like dogs do.

I run and I run, hoppin' over logs and stumps and low, muddy places and dodgin' 'round trees and palmettos. I slip through clusters of vines and weave through them roots my boy calls cypress knees. I'm goin' good, not breathin' too hard, not tired at all.

Soon enough, the levee widens out, and I know I'm gettin' closer to the open woods. There's a clear trail runnin' through a thick palmetto brake that I remember us comin' through, probly a deer trail. I start to pick up my boy's scent real strong as the path narrows, and that makes me feel good.

It makes me want to run faster, but then another smell slams me—a smell so strong and awful that it just about knocks me over.

I come skiddin' to a stop, my hackles risin'.

I whirl around, lookin' every which way, and find myself barkin' like I ain't ever barked before.

Up ahead, at the end of the trail, blockin' my way to the wide woods, is somethin' I cain't believe—a big, black horrible thing, reared way up, his head big as the softball my boy throws around in the yard sometimes.

His tongue flicks like a long flame in a campfire.

He don't say nuttin'. He just lowers his head and comes slitherin' my way.

I'm guessin' this is Pick.

When he gets about ten feet away, I whirl and run, headin' back the way I come. But as soon as I see an openin' in those palmettos, I dodge right into the palmetto thicket and double back, anglin' to try to put some distance between me and that path Pick's crawlin' on.

I wonder if this is such a good idea when my right front paw gets tangled in some vines and I go tumblin' and crashin' hard through those palmettos.

I scramble up and go runnin' forward, lookin' for the easiest way through. I see a path, the kind that might be made by raccoons, and I head for it. It's tight but clear for a good bit, and every foot I make gets me closer to the wide woods. Pick will see my backsides then.

Suddenly, though, that trail closes up and disappears altogether. I find myself at a dead end—up against a wall of twisted roots and vines that a mouse couldn't squeeze through.

Rascal, you idgit!

I feel like there's bees in my chest.

I double back, clawin' my way ahead, desperate, roots grabbin' at my paws, lookin' for a way out.

The trail opens up some, and I break into a gallop—only to see a big log blockin' my way.

I run even harder and jump over that log.

'Cept it ain't no log.

That smell rams into me again.

I've just jumped over Pick's big middle.

I've no sooner cleared him when there's a terrible thrashin' behind me.

I look back—a mistake—'cause I lose my footin' again and

go tumblin'. I bounce, head over heels, and land on my back. I'm lookin' behind me, only to see Pick come whippin' out of those palmettos—his head cocked back, his giant mouth wide open, his stinger glistenin' like ice on a knife.

He hisses loud as a teakettle.

I'm on my feet, a bit dizzy, my heart thumpin' fast as a rabbit. I don't have time to think. I just have to *do*.

Somethin' powerful comes over me—somethin' crazy— and I'm suddenly runnin' *toward* Pick, my fangs bared, a snarl comin' out of me that sounds like it comes from the Devil hisself.

My mind is tellin' me to be scared, but my body keeps runnin'. I'm snarlin' at that snake in a voice that don't sound like me. I hear myself sayin', "You may kill me, but I'm gonna make you pay—you'll never bite my boy. I'm comin' to break your neck!"

I'm about six dog lengths away from Pick when I'm stopped in my tracks.

Pick *roars*.

The stink on his breath is like bein' beat on the head with a log.

I've made an awful mistake.

Pick goes into a tight coil, his big, ugly mouth still open, his stinger stickin' out like a curved dagger, poison drippin' off the end.

"Look at me," he says in a voice as deep as the swamp it- self. "You're *so* dead."

He cocks his head, like he's thinkin' about what to do— and strikes.

I ain't ready.

His
big head comes
shootin' toward me bee-
quick. A jolt of fear sizzles
through my body. I jump, jump
like a starvin' dog tryin' to get
the world's last biscuit.

For a second, Pick's giant black
head sails right at mine.

He's all jaws and fang and stink,
and I close my eyes, waitin' for that stinger
to bury itself in my head.

*I'm sorry, Meely. I'm a stupid dog, lettin' myself
get caught like this.*

I'm waitin' to die—when I'm rocked by a sour wind as
the big lug's body whistles under me like God's own bullet.

I've jumped clean over him!

I feel like I'm floatin' in the air forever, then come down
hard—*thump!*—on Pick's big middle.

He roars again. It rattles my brain.

I'm tumblin' head over heels but land on my feet, heart
hammerin', the wind knocked out of me. I've landed at
Pick's tail end—he'd lunged so hard that he's stretched out
straight as a garden hose.

I see somethin' else—a scar zigzaggin' across his
broad back.

Big Maw wadn't lyin'—her claws raked him good.

Pick don't stay stretched out long. He lifts his head up, twistin' it around, and looks back at me with murder in them black snake eyes.

Cat-quick he's in a coil again. He may be stupid and slow to crawl—but he strikes fast as a gun-shot.

Somethin' in my deep dog brain tells me that if I run now, he'll get that stinger in my backside.

I got one other choice—another crazy choice.

I chomp down hard on the end of Pick's tail, feelin' bones crack as I do, and then I yank at him with all my might.

The hiss that comes out of him curdles my blood.

I start to run, bitin' harder, diggin' my paws into the ground like a mule tryin' to drag a loaded cane wagon. I taste bitter snake blood.

Maybe if I drag him fast enough, he won't be able to strike at me.

I know I've got this wrong when I look back and see Pick's big mouth come sailin' at me again.

I yank harder, diggin' my paws in deeper, divin' away from him, waitin' for this giant fang to cut through me like a poisoned arrow.

I don't care about livin' no more. I just want to hurt him as much as I can.

A growl boils out of me. I bite down like a snappin' turtle. I yank hard one more time—yank so hard with my whole body that I think my head might fly off.

I lunge ahead and Pick gives up some ground, and I hear what sounds like the crack of a whip.

I turn to look. Pick's awful head snaps back—snaps back so close to mine that I can smell the death on his breath.

"I'm gonna kill you!" Pick howls in his deep voice. "I'm gonna pump you so full of poison, the buzzards won't eat you!"

Pick's twistin' around for another strike, and it comes quick. But I ain't let him go. I yank again—yank like a dog fightin' over the world's last bone, scramblin' backwards all the time.

The world seems to slow down, and Pick's terrible head comes floatin' my way again.

Floatin', that milky dagger stickin' out, ready to bury itself in me.

I shut my eyes, then—*whack!* His head whipsaws back again.

I won't survive another strike.

My head goes fuzzy and my heart goes rabbity and there's a fire burnin' in my lungs and pain that feels like nails bein' driven into my legs. I don't care about dyin'.

It's only the voice of my boy in my head tellin' me I'm the only hope he's got that makes me give it one more shot. I lunge ahead, bitin' down so hard on Pick's tail that I could bite it in two, my paws diggin' deep into the dirt like a tractor, and suddenly I'm draggin' Pick's big ugly self across the ground—draggin' the monster backwards so that he cain't coil up proper for another strike.

The roar that comes outta him bangs into my skull like a hammer.

Up ahead, I spy my one chance—a closed-in rabbit trail runnin' through the palmettos.

I pick up speed, ignorin' the fire that's run from my legs into my chest and head, and drag Pick till I get to a place where the trail narrows to about the width of a dog.

I let go.

I glance over my shoulder and see the monster tryin' to twist hisself up for another strike. But the tight space gets him boxed in for just a second—and that's the second I need.

I gallop off, thinkin' about the bluetick in me, only hopin' this trail don't dead-end. Soon I spy a bigger openin' to my left.

I dart that way, and in no time I'm on the levee headin' in the general direction of Nonc's.

There's no Pick between me and the wide woods.

If my heart don't explode or my legs give out, I'm home free.

But I know this ain't true when I hear an awful thrashin' in the brush off to my side and see somethin' out the corner of my eye.

Pick comes streakin' up on me at an angle, tryin' to cut me off.

Who said he wadn't fast?

I know what he's runnin' on—he's runnin' on murder.

Soon we're almost side by side, Pick's giant mouth

snappin' open and shut. He hisses in a low rumble, "I got you now. I'm gonna bite you—then swallow you alive!"

Somethin' Big Maw would say pops into my head, and I yell, "You low-down, belly-crawlin', mud-suckin', night-creepin', cat-killin' coward! I hope you taste better to the buzzards than you did to me. Eat my dirt!"

There's fire in my lungs and my legs feel heavy as swamp mud, but I know this is it. If I slow down or stumble, I'm a goner.

Pick seems to know this, too.

He slows down, windin' tight into a coil for another strike.

I dig deep for my last burst of speed—I stretch out my gallop, runnin' blind, and it's as if I've left my body.

I feel like I'm floatin' above myself, watchin' myself run.

I don't see the strike this time—I feel it.

A blast of hot, stinky wind roars up from behind.

I look ahead. A palmetto thicket is blockin' my path. I leave my feet, jumpin' high as I can—but clip the top of a frond with my hind legs.

Suddenly I'm fallin', all twisted in the air, and I'm lookin' back, too beat to care if Pick gets me or not.

Pick's whole body comes sailin' at me.

And then a funny thing happens.

That palmetto frond I tripped over springs back upright.

There's a loud smack—*oof!*

Pick's big ugly head come punchin' through that palmetto like some giant arrow.

Snake blood splatters the air like rain.

Pick's groan fills up the woods.

And then it's Pick tumblin' through the air, makin' a big, twisty loop-de-loop, roarin' as he goes.

Somehow, before I hit the ground, I do a cat thing—I squirm myself over and land on my feet before I skid ahead toward a log blockin' my way.

Off to one side I hear a terrible sound—Pick bustin' through the bushes like a giant, drunk bird, snappin' off bush limbs as he goes.

Then—*thud*. The ground trembles as he crashes hard.

I smack right into that log with my head.

I'm dizzy. Things go black, but I know Pick ain't broke his fool neck 'cause somewhere in the foggy distance he wails again.

That wail runs like a nail through my head, and I'm back up on my feet and jumpin' over that log.

And Pick is screamin', "You lose, dog! I'm goin' back to get your boy. I know just where he is—I'm gonna pump him full of poison and suck out his eyes like eggs!!!"

I skid to a stop and whirl around, so mad that I just wanna go back and take a chunk outta Pick's throat no matter what happens.

But then the voice of my boy comes to me again clear in my head—"Get help, puppy. Go on."

I know that voice is right. My boy's got his gun and maybe Ole Swamp.

My job is to get Nonc.

I try not to think about how tired I am. I just run and run and run, pantin' like a racehorse, my tongue flopped out. I'm runnin' pretty much blind, followin' what looks like another deer trail, when the trail jogs hard 'round a big water oak.

I make that turn—and run smack into somethin'.

I'm yelpin'—and somethin' else is yelpin', too—and whatever it is, we're all tangled up together.

And suddenly I'm on my back, and I hear a fearsome growl that grows into an awful snarl.

Have I run clean into the paws of a swampcat?

I look up and there's a big dog standin' over me—teeth bared, about to take a bite out of my hide.

I yelp, "Don't—don't bite me! Don't, please! It's me— it's me, Rascal!"

Blackie Grand Baton is all hunched up over me, an awful look on his face.

But when he sees it's me, that look softens and his eyes get wide.

"Rascal? Rascal? Son, you scared the turnips outta me. What the heck you doin' runnin' crazy out here in this neck of the woods, ehn? Somethin' after you?"

Chapter 11

In the time that it takes me to catch my breath, I notice Blackie's not alone. There's a whole pack of dogs from Nonc's farm standin' 'round lookin' at me—Mamou, that big daddy deer dog, and yappy li'l ole Fuzzy. There's Belle and Beau and Midnight and that pretty dog, Sugarfoot.

She's lookin' at me good.

They're all pantin', like they've been runnin' hard, too.

I get my wind back and start tryin' to tell Blackie my mixed-up story. I get a bit in about my boy bein' stuck, but soon as the word *snake* comes out of my mouth, I hear Mamou growl.

"Where is he?" he says in a voice that sounds spooky as any dog's I've ever heard. "Where *is* that snake?"

I look up at him, but he ain't lookin' at me. He's lookin' off over my shoulder into the deep woods.

I'm about to answer when Blackie speaks up. "Rascal, we got big trouble. Mamou and Bon-Bon just had their puppies, and wouldn't you know it but a low-down, egg-suckin', night-crawlin' snake snuck into the farmyard late last night and killed one of the beauties—bit the sweet li'l puppy through the neck. By the time Bon-Bon and Mamou realized the puppy had been bit, the big ugly thang was crawlin' out through a hole it had punched in the pen. Mamou lunged at it, but that snake run off into the dark. Some of us from the yard went after it, but that devil had crawled off into the black of the cane field. Our ruckus woke ole Nonc.

115

He come out with a light and his shooter, but you know Nonc—only way he'da caught that snake is if he stepped on it. Anyway, us dogs have had enough. We've formed a posse, and we're gonna track that snake down and make it so he ain't never gonna crawl 'round our farm again. We know it's Ole Swamp—same snake that killed King before you was born. Same snake that killed Big Maw's kitty. He's a bad snake with bad poison, and some of us might not come back. But if we don't get him now, none of us will ever be able to sleep in peace again."

Blackie looks back at the other dogs. "Am I right, dogs? Even ole Tubby started out with us—though he's dropped back a fer piece."

Them dogs all nod.

Mamou speaks up again. "Where is he, Rascal? Where did you last see that murderin' snake?"

Mamou ain't never spoke my name before.

I nod back over my shoulder. "Back there a ways—he chased me all over kingdom come. I've just been runnin' and runnin' and runnin'. And, anyway, it ain't the snake you think it is. It ain't—it's—"

Mamou cuts me off. "I'm gonna kill him," he growls. "I'm gonna get that snake and chew him in half, I don't care what he does to me."

Then, before I can say another word, he's off, bawlin' through the woods like a thunderstorm.

"Can you go catch him?" I say to Blackie. "See, I was about to say there's two snakes, not one, that it ain't really Ole Swamp. It's another snake, a bigger snake, a worse snake, the baddest snake that's ever crawled in any woods anywhere. His name is Pick, and I don't think even big ole Mamou can tackle him by hisself. I—"

Blackie's just lookin' at me like I'm talkin' gibberish. "Rascal," he says, "what you mean? Everybody knows about Ole Swamp. Anyway, ain't no dog here gonna catch Mamou, not even me, and ain't no dog gonna be able to tell him nuttin'. He won't listen. But we'll die tryin' to help him catch that snake. Y'all ready, dogs?"

All the dogs start to bark and growl, and suddenly I feel like I've got bees swarmin' in my head again. This is all so hard to explain, 'specially to a bunch of stirred-up dogs.

"Look, Blackie, I'd go with you, but I cain't. I gotta try to get Nonc to come help my boy—I promised him. Y'all just follow my trail, and soon enough you should catch my boy's scent. Follow that and you'll have a good chance of runnin' into them snakes. And 'member, there's two, not one, and if you run into Pick, you'll know it 'cause he leaves a trail sour as what the buzzards eat. But watch out—he's a monster. He'll kill a dog easy as he'll look at one. If y'all hunt together, you might have a chance. If you get to my boy on that bridge, try to look after him till I get back, OK?"

Blackie looks at me, confused. "Whatever you say, Rascal. Good luck."

He turns to the other dogs. "If any dog wants to turn back, now's the time to do it. Once we're goin', we're in—no stoppin'."

I hear Sugarfoot bark. She looks at me, then says to Blackie, "I'm not afraid of any ole snake, but I wanna go with Rascal. I know the way back to Nonc's easy. It's a good ways, and he might need help gettin' there. He looks beat to

118

me. And if we gotta bark Nonc out of his house, better to have two dogs than one."

"Shore," says Blackie. "Do what you have to do, Sugar-foot. We got plenty of dogs here."

Then, Blackie throws his head back and howls, "Let's get that snake!"

He's off and runnin' with the rest of them dogs, and I'm hollerin' at him, "It's *two* snakes, Blackie. Two! And Pick's the snake you want—it ain't Ole Swamp!"

But them dogs are all off bawlin' and howlin', and I doubt they've heard a thing I've said.

"You ready, Rascal?" Sugarfoot says to me.

I nod.

"OK. I'll lead the way. You just tell me if I'm goin' too fast."

I think about my boy and feel somethin' stir in my tired bones.

"Don't worry," I say. "You run. I'll stay up."

Chapter 12

Me and Sugarfoot come into Nonc's pasture with our tongues hangin' out. She stops to lap up some water out of the cow trough. I'm parched as burnt corn bread, but I cain't stop.

I get up to the porch and start howlin'. Sugarfoot joins me quick.

We howl and howl and howl.

Nonc and Tante ain't hearin' us.

I jump up twice and throw my body against the front door, makin' a racket.

But nobody's comin'.

"What's *wrong* with them?" I say to Sugarfoot. "I know Nonc don't hear good, but that lady hears all right."

I see Sugarfoot lookin' around.

"Rascal, where's Nonc's ole green truck? I wadn't payin' much mind when we come in, but maybe Nonc and Tante have gone to town. That truck's always over there in front of the cypress garage, but it ain't there now."

I look that way and feel a wail startin' to crawl up in my throat. If Nonc really is gone, I've wasted my time runnin' all this way.

I might as well have stayed with my boy.

I look at Sugarfoot, and she sees what I'm thinkin'.

"Calm down, Rascal. Calm down. Maybe Nonc's gone, but maybe Tante's still in the house. Maybe if we try barkin' again, we can rouse her."

"For what?" I say. "She ain't gonna follow us back in the woods. She ain't got a shooter like Nonc does. She's not—"

"Rascal," says Sugarfoot, "if you want my opinion, Tante's the brains of this operation. If we can get her to the door, she'll figger somethin' out. Anyway, you got a better idea?"

I admit I don't.

She don't wait for me to answer. She puts her paws up on the front door and starts barkin' again like a crazy dog. I start barkin', too.

But in a few minutes we've barked ourselves out.

What am I s'posed to do now?

I wonder what Momma would do.

Then I have an idea.

"The road," I say. "I gotta go out on the road and get somebody to stop."

"The road?" says Sugarfoot. "That's crazy, Rascal. You know how them cane farmers drive—you know what happened to your poor momma. You'll just get yourself run over, and then your boy will really be in a fix."

"I'll watch out, but I gotta go. And if somethin' happens to me—well, you'll know what to do. You'll just wait here till Nonc gets back, and then you'll lead him to my boy."

Sugarfoot looks at me, shakin' her head. "I *don't* really know where your boy is, only what you've said. I might not know how to make it back there. No, I think you oughta just wait here with me. Nonc and Tante are never gone too long."

Sugarfoot's starin' at me with her big, bright brown eyes. I know she's only tryin' to look out for me, but she don't understand how it is 'tween me and my boy.

"I just cain't wait, Sugarfoot. I cain't. I'll be careful—I will."

As I turn to go, I hear her say, "Rascal, really, please. Don't go on the road. If anything should happen to you, I'd . . . well . . ."

I feel bad, but I don't even turn around.

I make it to the road in no time, but the problem is the road is empty. I trot out to the middle, where the shells have been piled by the comin' and goin' of trucks and cars, and look both ways but don't see a thing. I put my ear down to the road to listen for the rumble of one of them cane trucks.

The road's quiet.

I look back up toward Nonc's. Sugarfoot's up on the front porch, starin' at me.

My dog spirits go flat.

This is all *wrong*. My boy's out there by hisself, and I'm standin' here like a helpless fool.

I feel another wail comin' on, but I choke it back. I cain't go soft now. I start thinkin' 'bout what else I might do—could I run all the way to Miz Henrietta's and try to get her? She don't know the woods, but she's sweet on my boy and might figger out what to do.

It's a long way over there, and what if it turned out she's not home, either?

All this is startin' to make my dog brain go fuzzy when I hear—well, actually, feel—somethin'.

A rumble!

Nonc's farm sits on a straight stretch, and I look down the bayou in the direction of the rumble and see in the distance a truck throwin' up a good dust cloud behind it. It's gotta be one of them sugarcane trucks.

I haven't thought this through—the part about how to get the truck to stop. I don't think lyin' on the side of the road and chasin' it like Momma did will do any good.

No, I'll just have to sit here in the middle and hope the driver won't run over a dog if he can help it.

I turn to face the truck and watch it get bigger and bigger as the rumble gets louder and louder.

Soon, that truck is at a place where the driver should be seein' me—but it ain't slowed down a bit. I don't know what else to do, so I get up on my hind legs and I start barkin'.

That truck just keeps rumblin' on toward me.

The rumblin's so loud that it's startin' to hurt my ears.

The road's vibratin' under my feet.

The truck is draggin' a tornado of dust behind it.

Somethin' in me snaps—I know that the driver *don't* see me and *ain't* gonna slow down and I'm about five seconds from gettin' flattened just like my momma did.

I turn and bolt forward, the rumblin' gettin' louder and louder, turnin' into an awful, awful roar.

Then I hear somethin' else, a terrible screechin' and growlin' sound and then the loud blast of a horn.

I guess that fella sees me now.

Out of the corner of my right eye, I catch a flicker of black. Then somethin' slams into me, and I'm off my feet and tumblin' hard on the gravel.

I'm rollin' over and over and over, and I hear the terrible

roar of the truck go by. A shower of gravel peppers me like birdshot and I yelp out.

I'm flyin' through the air in a cloud of dust. I hit somethin' soft, and it takes a second to realize that I've tumbled off the road and down into the dirt of Nonc's bayouside garden.

And then somethin' slams into me again, knockin' the wind clear out of me. There's moanin' over behind me, and I'm lookin', tryin' to figger out what's happened.

Sugarfoot is layin', still as the day moon, on top of the next garden row.

Now I know what happened—she come runnin' and pushed me off the road, outta the way of that truck.

I'm hurtin' all over, but I pick myself up. I got a limp in my right paw, and my backsides sting from that gravel. I look back and see trickles of blood everyplace.

I hobble over to Sugarfoot and look down at her. Her eyes are closed and for a second I think she's done killed herself because of me, and I'm about to howl when I see that she's breathin'.

I start to lick her face like crazy, callin' her name over and over, and soon she opens her eyes and looks at me all soft.

"Oh, Rascal—is that you? Are you OK, Rascal?"

"Me? Yeah, I'm all right, but what about you? Sugarfoot, I'm sorry—I shoulda listened to you. That was stupid. I almost killed us both, I—"

I wanna say more, but Sugarfoot shushes me and rolls her eyes toward the road. Soon I know why.

I hear a man hollerin'—oh, he's hollerin' good. He's hollerin' and carryin' on like Nonc sometimes does, in Cajun French.

"*Chiens couillons! Chiens fous! Vous n'avez pas le sentiment que vous êtes né avec!* Y'all almost got me killed. What the heck you doin' runnin' 'round in the middle of the road like that? Dogs like you should be locked up. Who you belong to, ehn? I'm gonna go give 'em a piece of my mind!"

I look over and see a fella on the edge of the road in a straw hat and coveralls and boots. He's shakin' his fist at us. His cane truck is back behind him, turned sideways across the road.

The man's got a long stick in his hand, and I realize he ain't the kind of man who probly will help me.

I look at Sugarfoot, who's got to her feet.

She whispers, "You got any runnin' left in you, Rascal?"

Chapter 13

The man steps down into the garden with that stick raised and starts toward us.

Sugarfoot begins to ease away, lookin' over her shoulder, makin' sure we got a clear path if we have to run.

But I ain't runnin'. This man needs to understand that we ain't bad dogs, just dogs that got big trouble.

He comes closer, and I start to bark—a friendly bark.

He slows down and looks at me good. "What's wit' you, you crazy dog? Ain't you smart enough to know when you s'posed to run?"

He's still holdin' up that stick, and he's almost close enough to smack me with it.

I hear Sugarfoot off in the distance sayin', "Rascal, what you think you're doin'?"

I don't have time to explain.

I get up on my hind legs and bark again. I twirl around once, doin' the doggy dance I do when my boy gives me a biscuit. Then I come down on all fours and give him a couple of my best puppy whimpers.

The fella stops. He's shakin' his head, though he's still got that stick raised. "What? You sorry? Is that what you're tryin' to tell me? You're sorry you almost made me run my cane truck off this road and into the bayou?"

I get back up on my hind legs and bark twice, "Yes, yes!"

He's still shakin' his head, tryin' to decide what to do,

when I hear a horn blowin' loud and then somebody else is hollerin'.

The man looks off in the direction of the sound, and I hear a door slam. 'Cause I'm low down in the garden, I cain't see nobody yet, but I hear boots crunchin' across the gravel road.

Then I hear a voice I know—Nonc!

"Claude Naquin," Nonc says. "What on eart' you doin' standin' yuh in my garden wit' your truck blockin' the road raisin' heck wit' some dogs, ehn?"

The fella lowers his stick and turns toward Nonc's voice. He gives Nonc an earful.

"Good thing I was runnin' empty 'cause otherwise I never woulda stopped in time. If my trailer had been loaded wit' cane, that beagle would be dead and I'd be sunk down there in the bayou someplace, probly dead myself. You need to watch after your dogs."

I still cain't see Nonc, and it's plain he cain't see me when he says, "What beagle you talkin' about? The onliest beagle I got in my yard is a big ole fat stud dog. He's a good dog, but he's a lazy so-and-so. He won't chase a rabbit, much less a truck."

The man points at me. "I'm talkin' 'bout this li'l beagle right yuh. And that black mutt wit' him—the one wit' the white foot. The beagle was layin' up in the middle of the road, and that black dog come chasin' right clear across my path."

Next thing I know, Nonc's skinny self is at the edge of the garden lookin' down at me. I see him make a face. Tante walks up behind him. She's shadin' her eyes, lookin', too.

"Well, I'll be John Brown," says Nonc. "It's that Rascal dog—back again. I give him away some months back to the boy who lives wit' my niece up the bayou. He could get into some mischief now and then, but he wadn't a bad dog and he wadn't no truck chaser. That li'l black dog, neither. I don't understand what they was doin' in the road. That beagle and that boy—my niece says they stuck on each other like a spider and a web. You didn't see no boy around, did you, Claude?"

"No, Noon, wadn't nobody around that I could see."

Nonc shakes his head. "Somethin' about this ain't right."

"*Mais*, Noon," says Claude, "maybe not, but I know what I saw. I ain't crazy and my truck didn't end up like this 'cause I forgot how to drive while I was passin' by your house. What, you think I'm tellin' you a story?"

Nonc waves his hand at Naquin. "*Mais, non*, Claude. I believe everything you said. I just don't understand what's goin' on wit' these dogs. It ain't like neither one of 'em."

"Maybe they're *craque*," says Claude. "They shore acted like they was. Maybe they caught that rabies."

Nonc shrugs. "Claude, Claude, them dogs ain't got no rabies—you see 'em foamin' at the mouth? Shuh."

He steps down into the garden and comes toward me.

I look at Sugarfoot and she looks at me. She's thinkin' what I'm thinkin'.

We don't let Nonc get to us. We go racin' right toward him, barkin' like crazy—worried barkin', but Nonc don't seem to know the difference.

"Whoa, whoa, whoa, dogs," he says, backin' up. "Nonc ain't comin' to hurt y'all. Just calm down."

"You want my stick?" says Naquin.

Me and Sugarfoot stop runnin'—we don't want to scare Nonc off—though we keep barkin', and hoppin' up and down, too.

Then Tante speaks. "Beb," says Tante Lo-Lo, "you don't need no stick. Them dogs don't wanna bite you. They tryin' to tell you somethin'."

"Tryin' to tell me somethin'? What, you speak dog? You know what they sayin'?"

"No, I don't speak dog, but somethin's goin' on, I can tell you that much."

Sugarfoot looks at me and whispers, "I told you, Rascal. Tante's the one with the brains."

I nod at that. I just don't know what to do now.

Bark some more?

Try to run and get Nonc to follow me?

Tante speaks up again. "Noon, I think you were right earlier 'bout what you said—that it ain't right that Rascal and that boy ain't together. I think we need to go inside and call your niece, Henrietta. If it turns out that dog has run off, she'll want to know. But, me, I don't think that's what's goin' on."

Nonc looks at Tante and then looks back at us. "OK, that's a good idea." Then he looks at Claude.

"Claude, podnah, I'm sorry 'bout you awmost wreckin'. Why don't you pull your truck up straight on the shoulder and come in and get some coffee? Tante will fix up a pot while I call my niece."

"Aw, Noon, there ain't nuttin' I'd like more than a good, strong cup of coffee. But I gotta make two more runs to the sugar mill before dark. If I ain't at the loadin' dock down there at Hebert's Farm in twenty minutes, ole Usie Daigle, the overseer, is gonna be jumpin' up and down like the *roogarou*."

Nonc nods. "Awright, podnah. Drive safe."

Claude laughs at that. "Yeah, well, I will if I ain't attacked by no more crazy dogs."

He turns and trudges up the garden bank and heads for his truck.

Nonc looks at Tante. "You pull the pickup into the driveway, beb, while I go call Henrietta."

"Awright," says Tante. She looks at me and Sugarfoot.

"Vien ici, chiens," she says. "Y'all hop up in the back of the truck. Me, I think we're goin' for a ride someplace, though I don't know where."

I look at Sugarfoot again, and then I find myself doin' a funny thing. I know Tante has still got it in for me for chasin' her chickens, but I go runnin' up to her and before she knows it, I've jumped clean up and given her a big lick on the face.

I hit the ground barkin', bouncin' up and down again.

Tante *understands* me! She *knows* somethin's wrong!

She stumbles back some and wipes her cheek where I licked her. I can tell that she don't know whether to laugh or be cross. She looks at me like she wants to fuss me, but then she says, not in a mean way, *"Fais pas ça,* you crazy li'l dog. Get up in that truck and behave yourself."

She takes a couple of steps and opens the tailgate. I hop in quick.

She looks at Sugarfoot and says, "You, too."

Sugarfoot comes runnin' and jumps up beside me. Tante shuts the tailgate and climbs into the truck. By the time we make it to the ole cypress garage, Nonc's come out the front door.

"We might got some trouble, beb. Henrietta says Meely and that dog took off early this mornin' to go squirrel huntin' over in them big woods back of Cancienne's corn patch. He ain't back yet, which is unusual 'cause he almost always comes back in time for his dinner. And now his dog is back wit'out him."

Tante nods. "Well, I told you, Noon, that beagle was tryin' to tell you somethin'. If you ax me, I'm bettin' that boy's stuck out there someplace and that beagle's come back to find some help."

Then I see Tante make the sign of the cross. "*Mais*, I hope nuttin' bad has happened to him. He seems like a very good boy—Henrietta loves him to death."

"Oh yeah. Henrietta was plenty worried and wants to call the sheriff to come out and look for him. But, shuh, I told her that by the time she gets them ole boys on the trail, it'll be dark, so I better go look myself. I've hunted them woods a time or two and know that stretch perty good. And, anyway, if I ain't back by dark, y'all maybe better send the police after me."

"Well, Noon, now you scarin' me. I don't want you to get yourself lost out there, no."

Nonc bats the air like he's battin' away a mosquito. "Aw, don't you worry 'bout me. Besides, I'm gonna take these dogs, and maybe a couple others."

Nonc puts two fingers in his mouth and gives a loud dog whistle.

I guess he's expectin' dogs to come, but I know his dogs,

'cept for that momma dog Bon-Bon and her puppies, are all out in the woods huntin' that snake. Even fat ole Tubby.

When no dogs come trottin' up, he whistles again and then again. Ain't a dog stirrin'.

"What the heck is goin' on?" says Nonc. "Where the heck's them dogs? They're always here when I feed 'em. Where they at when I need 'em?"

Tante shrugs. "*Mais*, I dunno, me."

Nonc shakes his head. "Somethin' ain't right. Anyway, I better get goin'. We ain't got more than three hours of daylight lef', and it could be a long way out there."

"Well, take your bulleye, Noon, 'case you get caught in the dark. And take some water and some food. And your gun—that big ole shotgun you got—and plenty of bullets. Somethin' bad comes after you, you shoot it, beb—shoot it good."

"Aw, Lo-Lo, ain't nuttin' out there I cain't handle. And, anyway, look what I got guardin' me—a half-growed beagle that knows everything I'm sayin' and a sugar-footed mutt that tried to run a cane truck off the road. I'll be awright."

"That ain't funny, Noon. What if you run into that *roogarou*, ehn?"

"Lo-Lo, don't start wit' the *roogarou*. You know that swamp werewolf ain't real—that's a story your maw-maw used to tell you to make you behave when you was bein' a bad girl. My maw-maw told me the same story."

"That's what you say, Noon, but I saw that thing one night when I was a chile. I know it's out there."

Tante crosses herself again.

I look at Sugarfoot. These people could talk a ham off a hog.

"Lo-Lo, you didn't see no such thing. You dreamt that. I been all over these woods and ain't seen nuttin' close to the *roogarou*. I ain't even seen a real wolf. Close as I could come is a bobcat one time."

"That's like a tiger, ain't it, Noon?"

I can see Nonc's gettin' tired of talkin', too.

"*Mais, non*, woman. A bobcat is just an overgrowed barn cat. The one I saw probly wadn't bigger than that momma cat that stays over in the barn. Anyway, don't worry, Lo-Lo. I'll be back in time to eat my gumbo. Be easy on the cayenne tonight, all right? Now, I gotta get my stuff so we can get goin'."

I'm barkin' loud at that. "Hurry up, Nonc! Hurry up!"

Nonc looks at me. "Keep your fur on, puppy. I'm goin' fast as I can."

I just hope it's fast enough.

Chapter 14

We're in the deep woods, and I'm a fidgety dog.

I thought we'd never make it. Nonc drove along some bumpy dirt roads windin' through the sugarcane fields to get to the spot where Meely and me entered the woods. His old truck coughed and sputtered and grumbled the whole way.

Spanish moss grows faster than Nonc's been movin'.

He's all kitted out and he's fiddlin' with everything—his gun, his vest, a hatchet he's hung from his belt, his canteen. He keeps droppin' this and that.

He's already slung his bulleye around his cap, but it keeps droopin' and gettin' way down around his eyes.

He keeps cussin' it.

I've trotted ahead tryin' to pick up my boy's scent, but I ain't found it yet.

Sugarfoot's come up to help, and we're sniffin' like crazy.

"It's gotta be here," I tell her. "Why ain't I gettin' it? I'm sure we walked this way."

"Try a wider circle," says Sugarfoot.

I know that's good advice, but I'm annoyed and she sees that. "Calm down, Rascal. Keep your nose down and you'll find it."

I start another big circle, sniffin' and sniffin' and sniffin'.

It just ain't to be found, and I'm so mad at myself that I'm about to howl when I strike it—*owwwrooooooh!*

Sugarfoot scrambles over.

"Got him, Rascal?"

"I do. Sniff good right here. You need to know what he smells like in case we get separated."

She sniffs careful.

"OK, I got it," she says. "Your boy smells good. Not like Nonc—he's kinda sour, ain't he?"

"Kinda? Nonc smells like a possum to me."

"That's funny, Rascal. Funny but true."

We look back. Nonc's just comin' into sight, still fussin' with his equipment.

At this rate, we ain't never gonna get to my boy. I know what I've got to do—run ahead, and fast, too.

"You stick with Nonc," I tell Sugarfoot, "and keep him on my trail. OK?"

Sugarfoot looks at me deep. I can see in her eyes that she's frettin', too. "Well, OK, Rascal. But what if I lose your trail? What if we wander off in the wrong direction? You might find your boy quick, but if Nonc don't come to get him out, you'll still be in a fix."

I shake my head. "You won't get lost. You're a good

tracker—look how easy you led me to Nonc's. Just go steady but not so fast that you wear the ole fella out."

"OK, I'll try. Go on—and be careful. Watch out for them bad ole snakes."

I look back. Nonc's finally caught up to us. I stand and bark and then dart off in the direction of Meely's scent. Then I double back and bark some more.

"That way?" says Nonc, pointin' toward me.

I howl, "Yes, yes, yes!" and start to run that way, glancin' back to make sure Nonc's lookin' at me.

Nonc looks down at Sugarfoot. "OK, pooch. I'm followin' y'all."

I light out, goin' as quick as I can and still keep Meely's smell. I can hear Nonc grumblin' as I pull away—"Slow down, slow down, doggone you!"

A dog feels bad when he don't listen, but I cain't slow down.

I run on and on, but trackin' my way back to my boy ain't as easy as I figgered. The scent gets better, but there's spots where it disappears altogether. I hit a low patch where there's some puddles across the trail and I run out of smell altogether.

Where could it be?

I sniff and sniff and sniff around the edges of the puddle. No scent.

I feel a howl comin' on. Where has it gone? Where?!

I try another circle and spy some sloppy footprints through a puddle—there he is!

Then I think about Sugarfoot. What if she gets stumped here, too?

I run back fast across those puddles and roll around good

in the mud on the other side. She'll smell that for sure. I roll clear across the puddle to the other side.

I'm a wet, muddy mess, but a blind dog ought to be able to track me across them puddles.

I shake myself off, mud and water flyin' every which way, and light out again.

I run on and on, keepin' my nose close to the ground. Soon enough, my boy's scent is plenty strong, so I can pick up my pace. I come to a spot where there's a clear trail ahead of me, and the smell gets stronger than ever.

I suddenly know where I am—this is the last stretch of open woods before I hit the levee that will lead me back to the bridge where my boy is stuck.

I don't need my nose anymore. I can just run, run, run!

I howl like I ain't never howled before.

I try to go quicker, but my dog body won't listen. I'm pantin' hard. My bones hurt and my muscles feel like red aints is gnawin' on 'em.

Soon enough, I make the levee. The trail narrows here. I'm pickin' up strong dog smells, so many that I cain't tell one dog from the other.

But that means the farmhouse posse has come this far—maybe they've already got to my boy!

I clip along as best I can, though the runnin' gets hard. I gotta hop over logs and dodge palmettos and vines and roots and such. I stumble a coupla times. I get nipped by briars that cut at my legs.

I round a small bend, and suddenly I hear somethin'—a faraway sound. I skid to a stop, tryin' to make out the direction over the drummin' of my heart.

It's up ahead, and I know what it is—it's a whole pack of dogs bawlin' up a hurricane.

A bad feelin' comes over me. Somethin' about it ain't right.

Has somethin' happened to my boy?

I light out, goin' hard, runnin' blind toward the sound, stumblin', crashin' through palmettos, pickin' myself up, runnin' on till the bawlin' gets louder and louder. I dart through a palmetto thicket, catch a root, and go tumblin', skiddin' plumb off the levee clear into a patch of swamp water.

I pick myself up, dizzy, and listen.

Them dogs are howlin' close.

I look toward the racket—and there they are, the whole mess of 'em, standin' 'round a big stump just a trot away. Mamou and lanky Blackie have got their heads back, bawlin' like they've treed the Devil hisself.

I charge over, splashin' through the shallow water, barkin' loud as I can. "Blackie!" I yell. "Blackie! What's goin' on here, Blackie?"

All them dogs got their backs to me, and nobody hears me.

I go runnin' through the middle of them, tryin' to get to Blackie. I run into a coupla them dogs and spook 'em.

One of 'em yelps and even takes a nip at me as I go by. I don't even look back.

I skid right through the pile, runnin' into Blackie, bouncin' off his long back legs.

He yelps and jumps up in the air and whirls around to bite the thing he thinks is attackin' him.

140

He bumps into Mamou, who growls fierce as he tries to jump out of the way.

I slide under both them big dogs and into that stump.

I hit hard with my back—*oof!*

I'm layin' there, belly-up, and see Blackie and Mamou about to go after each other. Then, one of them other dogs sees me and starts howlin'.

"Don't! Don't! Don't fight. It's just Rascal! It's Rascal!"

Blackie and Mamou look toward that li'l dog like they might bite his head off first, but then Blackie sees me.

"Rascal?" he says. "Doggone it, son, you gone crazy as a cat? You almost caused a dogfight."

I look at Mamou, who's still got fight in his eyes. But he ain't lookin' at Blackie. He's lookin' at me.

I roll over and get to my feet. "Sorry, y'all," I say. "I didn't mean to spook everybody. I just wanted to find out what the barkin' was all about. I, uh—"

Mamou interrupts me, all growly. "What the barkin' is all about is that yellow-bellied, mud-suckin', puppy-killin' snake has done crawled into a hole in this stump. I almost got him by the tail, but he slipped in there before I could get my jaws on him. Now that coward that kilt my baby won't come out. I've done told him I'd fight him fair—fang to fang. But he ain't so brave when it's somebody his own size that wants to fight. Did you bring Nonc? Does he have his shooter? Maybe he could stick it in that hole and blow this snake to smithereens."

I'm takin' this all in, and a bad feelin' comes over me.

"Mamou, how big is this snake?"

"A monster—six foot at least."

"Did he have a scar on his tail?"

"A scar? I dunno, Rascal. I was too busy tryin' to bite him in two to notice. Who cares?"

"Show me the hole he crawled in."

He jerks his head to the side. "It's there, the one up on the stump a bit."

I look and see that hole—and I know there's no way that Pick coulda squeezed in there.

A *frisson* of anger comes over me.

I call out, "Ole Swamp? Swamp? Are you in there? Swamp, it's Rascal. You gotta tell me if you are. 'Cause if you're in there, it means there ain't nobody protectin' my boy from Pick."

Mamou looks at me like I *am* crazy as a cat.

"C'mon, Swamp," I say louder. "If it's you, you need to tell me. I'll get these dogs to leave you alone. I've fetched the Two-Footer from the farm, and he's comin' up behind me with his shooter. You don't want to be in there when he gets here. You know he ain't like my boy when it comes to snakes."

There's still no answer, and I find myself gettin' madder than a stepped-on bee. I go over to that hole and peep in and start clawin' at it with all my might.

I hear Blackie holler, "Rascal, don't! If that snake's in there, he'll—"

But he shushes when a voice comes from somewhere deep in that stump.

"Rascal," says the voice, "I tried to tell that big, ugly dog that he had the wrong snake, but the big, dumb fool wouldn't listen. I could smell Pick sneakin' 'round, and I set a trap to teach his mean self a lesson when this hound come bawlin' in like a hurricane and flushed me from the levee. I had no choice but to run. 'Course, since he's a dog and dogs ain't got no sense, he just *had* to chase me. Just like the rest of the fools followin' him. They've messed up, big-time, Rascal, 'cause Pick's here. I smelled him—he was stinkin' up the woods like a fire."

I look at Mamou and Blackie, and I would be fightin' mad, 'cept I see a certain look in Blackie's eyes.

I shake my head. "It's the wrong snake, y'all. And now my boy's stuck on that bridge down at the end of the levee, and there's nobody 'tween him and the bad snake that wants to kill him."

Blackie don't say a thing. He just turns and starts to run back toward the levee, howlin' like a mad dog.

I light out after him, howlin', too, my heart beatin' like thunder in my ears.

Chapter 15

The run is a blur—big Mamou chargin' past me and Blackie like some devil dog, his feet barely touchin' the ground, his voice fillin' up the woods with a wail that might scare any snake but Pick.

I fall behind Blackie.

I stumble, I howl, I cuss myself for bein' so slow. I cuss my tired legs.

I run blind, fire in my chest, and the onliest thing that keeps me runnin' is a picture in my head of my boy, helpless on that bridge, Pick's hateful self crawlin' toward him.

I hear Mamou's wail way up ahead and a hurricane of bawlin' dogs comin' up from behind.

I hit a straight stretch—and look up just in time to see Blackie stopped dead up ahead of me.

I dive to my left to keep from runnin' up his backsides. I skid around him sideways like that cane truck that almost run me down.

I know why Blackie's stopped—we're at the bridge!

I look back and I ain't never seen a 'dog look so mad—Blackie's eyes are filled with fire, his fangs bared, a rumbly growl comin' from deep inside.

"Whuh—what, Blackie? Whuh—what's goin' on?"

He nods ahead.

I look. My blood curdles like sour milk.

Mamou is out on the bridge, about halfway to my boy.

Between him and Meely is Pick—reared up so he's about eye level with Mamou, his ugly ole mouth wide open, his stinger catchin' the sun slantin' through the cypresses.

My boy's eyes is closed. His shooter is propped in the crook of his arm.

He ain't movin'.

"Let's go!" I whisper to Blackie. "Let's go get that snake! Let's go help Mamou! I gotta get to my boy—now!"

"Hold it, Rascal, hold it," Blackie says in a low voice. "That bridge ain't wide enough for all of us. If we go out there now, we'll just distract Mamou, and he don't need no distractions. You see the size of that monster? He's done struck at Mamou twice. He's quicker than a scalded fox and packin' a mule's kick—not to mention that stinger. No, it's Mamou's fight now, and we gotta let him fight it out."

"But there ain't *time*, Blackie. I gotta go see 'bout my boy. He ain't movin'. He needs me. What if—what if—?"

An awful thought washes over me.

What if that snake's already bit him?

What if he's layin' there with poison oozin' through his veins?

Blackie seems to read my mind. "Now, calm down, pup. Your boy's alive, I know that much. I saw him move when Mamou first went out there on that bridge to bark at that snake."

I look at Blackie, wonderin' if he's tellin' me the truth.

If I could, I'd run right at Pick and let him bite me, and then I'd bite him like he ain't never been bit.

I'd crush his ugly snake bones before I died.

I feel helpless—I feel sick.

"Blackie, I hope you're right. But let's get closer. What if that snake gets the best of Mamou? We gotta be ready to move—move quick."

Blackie looks at me deep, then whispers, "Oh, I'm ready, Rascal. I'm plenty ready. See, I don't wanna move too close, give that snake any ideas. He thinks he's safe out there, but he ain't. I got my nootra move all lined up."

I look at beat-up ole Blackie.

I'm just glad to see fire in his eyes. I hope it's fire enough.

We look out toward the bridge again. Mamou is down in a crouch, his head weavin' slow in time with that snake's. Then Pick lifts his head up higher.

He sees us.

"Well, the cavalry has arrived," he spits in that deep, hissy voice of his. "I hope there's a lot more of you than that pitiful ole bag of mange and that pitiful puppy that I already chased outta these woods."

He looks straight at me.

"When I'm done with this miserable hound here, I'm comin' to finish my business with you, dog. Well—after I bite that boy. So get ready."

A howl jumps outta me before I can stop it. "You creep!" I bark. "I already took one bite outta your nasty hide. I—"

"Shush, Rascal!" Blackie says. "Don't talk to him. It'll only stir him up. It'll—"

Blackie's words don't hardly leave his mouth when I see Mamou take his eyes off that snake to look up at us.

I've done an awful thing.

Pick strikes like a rifle shot—*smack!*

Mamou's head jerks up and his eyes roll backwards.

He tries to get up out of his crouch, but he's all wobbly, like he's been hit in the head by a board.

He snarls, his mouth wide open, and he bites hard, dog slobber flyin' every which way, but he only bites air.

That snake hits him again—*thud*—this time square up against his ear.

Mamou's head snaps back, and a howl comes tumblin' out of him, then dies just as quick.

He goes limp, loses his legs, rolls.

Mamou falls off the bridge.

There's a giant splash as he hits the water.

Me and Blackie are stuck to that levee like dead bugs in a sticky trap.

"One down, three to go," says Pick. "Oh, and I didn't bite that dog—just smacked him silly. I'm savin' my poison for the rest of you. But, first, the boy."

A howl jumps outta me that shakes my own brain, and I'm suddenly runnin' full speed for that bridge. My paws hit wood and I slip-slide sideways, thinkin' for a second that I'm goin' over the side with Mamou.

But I dig hard and right myself and then leap toward the trailin' end of Pick's tail.

I know I've made the worst mistake of my life when I see Pick whirl back quick as a bat. He whips into a tight coil— then slings his entire body right at me.

The world slows down again, and I'm just tryin' to think of what I can do to hurt him before he stabs me deep with that stinger.

I see his giant milky white mouth floatin' my way.

I see that dagger drippin' with venom.

I want to shut my eyes but I cain't.

Then I see somethin' else—somethin' unbelievable.

A big gray blur comes divin' like a hawk outta the air.

It comes wailin' like the meanest hellcat that ever roamed any swamp—claws like long, bent nails ready to rip and tear.

It comes with fangs shinin' like the sun off a metal spoon.

Big Maw comes divin' out of the trees above us.

She lands—*whomp*—on Pick's broad back and digs her front claws deep into him. Her back claws rake and tear his scaly flesh. Blood flies everyplace.

Pick's stench staggers me as his giant head snaps back a breath from mine.

I see surprise in his hateful eyes.

Big Maw's spittin' at him—"You stinkin', low-down, yellow-bellied, night-creepin', baby-killin' coward. Go meet the Devil that made you!"

She sinks her big fangs into his back.

Pick whirls and his scream fills up the woods. "You're dead, cat! Deeeeeeead!"

And then it happens—Pick strikes, and his fang stabs deep into Maw's hind leg.

Maw flinches but she don't cry out. She bites down harder on Pick's back. Her back claws rake at him like a chain saw.

Pick shrieks.

Some horrible stink pours out of him.

He jerks that stinger out and rears back for another strike.

He roars in some crazy snake language.

From behind me there's a commotion.

. Somethin' strikes the back of my head, and I yelp—wonderin' if I'm bein' attacked by another snake.

But it ain't a snake—it's Blackie!

His hind foot clips me as he goes sailin' over my head, his long body stretched out, his jaws wide open.

He lands with a heavy skitterin' of paws and without missin' a beat lunges forward with all his might.

Pick's second strike is about halfway to Maw when Blackie's jaws close 'round his neck just behind his giant head.

Bones crunch.

Blackie shakes his head fierce, so fierce that I fear his eyeballs might pop out of their sockets.

Then, *snap!!!!*

Pick's head goes all jerky. His snake eyes flutter like a butterfly.

He tries desperate to turn back on what's got him, his stinger spewin' poison like a punctured garden hose.

Blackie lands with a thud, his paws diggin' hard into them bridge planks as he tries to stop hisself.

But Blackie's goin' too fast.

The whole mess of 'em—Blackie, Pick, and Big Maw, her claws still deep in that snake—go tumblin' in a big ole knot over the side.

And then every sound in the entire world disappears.

Chapter 16

I'm tryin' to howl, tryin' to think what on earth I might do, when I hear a sound.

It's a voice—my boy's voice.

It's soft, not at all like my boy's voice usually is, but he says, "Rascal, did I just see what I think I saw?"

I don't know where to run first, so I run to my boy, lickin' his face like he ain't never been licked before.

He pats my head and kisses my nose. "Rascal, mighty dog, you've come back. Did you bring Nonc with you?"

I bark that I have, even if Nonc ain't made it here yet.

Then I howl. I howl out Sugarfoot's name, tellin' her to come quick, hopin' she's close enough to hear me.

My boy don't look so good—pale. He's got circles under his eyes.

"I thought I was dreamin', Rascal," he says. "I thought that big snake was just a bad dream. I must've passed out for a while."

There's some splashin' below. I squeeze 'round my boy to look over the edge of the bridge.

It's Blackie, paddlin' his way slow toward the bank, towin' Big Maw by the scruff of her neck.

Maw's moanin' low.

Pick's giant body floats nearby, his white belly to the sky, his head bent like a broke stick.

Blood slicks the water around him.

Suddenly there's the groanin' of a dog on the other side of the bridge.

It's Mamou. He's clawed his way to shallow water up against the bank, but he don't look so good, either.

I bark and he turns to look at me. "I'm hurt, Rascal," he says. "My hip bone—I think it's broke. I landed on a stump or somethin' hard. I doubt I can get up this bank."

I wanna go help Mamou when I hear Blackie barkin' out, "Rascal, come down here, pup. I need some help to get this big ole cat up the bank."

What's a dog s'posed to do?

"Mamou, you just hold on," I yell out. "I gotta go help Blackie with Maw, then I'll try to help you."

I squeeze back 'round my boy and run off the bridge, cuttin' down the steep bank. I'm suddenly slip-slidin' and then I'm fallin', and it's all I can do to squirm my body so I don't fall on Blackie and Big Maw at the bottom.

I tumble into the shallow water next to them and come up sputterin'.

Blackie's done towed Maw to the water's edge and laid her so her head's on the soft, muddy bank.

"Now, you would have to be the biggest doggone cat that ever lived, wouldn't you?" says Blackie.

Maw's got her eyes closed. But she says, "And you would have to be a sorry ole pitiful mange rug, wouldn't you?"

"Well, I might be. But I towed your snakebit self to this bank, didn't I, lady? And some dogs that you took a chunk out of some time ago mighta not done such a thing."

Maw still don't bother openin' her eyes. "I took a chunk outta you 'cause you come creepin' 'round my house without bein' axed in. What's a cat s'posed to do, ehn? Let every Tom, Dick, and Rover come mussin' 'round where they ain't s'posed to?"

"Well, that barn door was open, and, anyway, I ain't never bit no cat nor ever wanted to. I was just in there seein' what I could see. I wadn't lookin' for no trouble."

"As if. You come in lookin' for a fight."

"You're just crazy—like most cats."

Maw opens her eyes and looks at me. "Do you hear this dog, Rascal? Insultin' me and my kind when he knows I cain't fight back. You just tell him he don't have to carry Maw nowhere. I'll figger a way outta here."

"I ain't insultin' her, Rascal," says Blackie. "I'm just tellin' the dog's own truth. Anyway, it ain't a lie to say she's big. I was so hungry once I tried to steal a whole sack of potatoes off a fella's porch, and she's heavier than that. We might need a lot more dogs than us to drag her up this bank."

"That's all I need," says Maw. "A bunch of dogs chewin'

on me tryin' to get me up the bank. Just let Maw lay here for a while. Maw's gonna be fine."

"She won't be," says Blackie. "That durned snake got her good. Look at her leg. It's already swole up like a melon."

I look and see Blackie's tellin' the truth. It's an awful sight.

I don't know what to do. I wanna howl again but I don't want to rile Maw up.

I say, "How you feelin', Maw? Does that leg hurt?"

"I've felt better, Rascal. Actually, I cain't feel that leg at all. But at least I'm doin' better than that nasty ole snake. I surprised his ugly self, didn't I, pup? Well, I guess we both did—me and this mange rug here."

"Maw," I say, "you saved my boy and me, and then Blackie saved you. That snake was comin' back for another bite."

"Shuh," she says. "I wadn't tryin' to save nobody, Rascal. I just wanted to show that snake he wadn't the boss—that he couldn't keep comin' 'round our farm and killin' our babies 'cause he likes to. I got no truck with them deer dogs, but when I heard 'bout that poor puppy, my blood turned cold. Cold, I'm tellin' you. Them dogs all lit out in a huff, like dogs do—not one of 'em even stopped to ax Maw for her help, though every dog knows I lost a baby to that snake, too. But I went slippin' through the woods after them. Oh no, Maw wadn't gonna be left out. No way."

Then I hear Maw breathe funny, and she closes her eyes again. She says, "Are you cold, Rascal? It's cold here."

Blackie looks hard at Maw, though he ain't lookin' in a mean way. He says to me, "Now, why would we wanna ax that mean ole cat to help us out, Rascal, when she ain't never got a good thing to say about a dog? Well, 'cept maybe you and your poor momma."

"Well, there you go, puppy," says Maw. "Mange rug here makes my point. The only two *polite* dogs with manners in that whole farmyard was you and your late momma, God bless her. And, oh, well, I'll throw in lazy ole Tubby. Them's that show respect gets respect—you know what Maw's sayin' is the gospel."

"Respect works both ways," says Blackie. "A cat who just got her hide saved by a dog might have somethin' more to say than callin' that dog a mange rug. What you think about that, Rascal?"

I gotta shake my head at all this. Maw needs to be savin' her strength to beat that snake poison, and Blackie needs to be savin' his to get Maw up this steep bank.

"I think y'all are both right, but let's save this talkin' for later, OK? We gotta get Maw outta here."

"And then what, Rascal?" says Maw. "Mr. Blackie here's gonna drag me by the scruff of my neck all the way back to the farm? Carry me on his back? Now, Maw might agree that he might *not* be the worst dog ever. But it's true—I'm probly the biggest cat that God ever made. Ain't a dog I ever seen strong enough to carry Maw all that way."

"Did you hear that, Rascal? She called me Mr. Blackie. Now we gettin' somewhere."

He looks at Maw. "We'll see just how far this mange rug can get you. Now, you just hold still as possible. Rascal, I'm gonna grab her by the scruff of the neck again and start up. You try to push with your nose on the backside."

"No, no, no," says Maw. "That ain't gonna work. Rascal, you just grab Maw by the tail and pull when Mr. Blackie does. It ain't gonna hurt this ole cat, and that's the only chance y'all got."

"OK by me," says Blackie. "It ain't my tail Rascal will be chewin' on."

"Hah," says Maw. "Listen to him—he's even got a sense of humor."

"Shush, Big Maw," I say soft. "Let's get you up there."

Me and Blackie latch on and start tuggin' hard, our feet slip-slidin' in the soft bank. We get her 'bout halfway up when Blackie's legs go out from under him and he tumbles backwards, draggin' Maw with him. They're both suddenly fallin' on top of me, and we all go tumblin' with a splash back into the shallow water.

I scramble to my feet to see Maw lyin' on her side, her face still underwater. Her body is all trembly as she's tryin' to right herself. Blackie picks hisself up, and we both scramble over to her. This time, I grab her by the scruff of the neck and drag her head out of the water.

I hear Blackie sayin', "Oh, I'm sorry, big cat. I'm sorry. I know what you think about me, but I didn't mean to do that. We'll give it another try. We'll—"

"Don't," Maw sputters as she spits out water. "Don't bother. Maw knows what the deal is. I can feel that poison movin' on up my body. Even if you get me up there on that bank, I ain't gonna make it."

"No, Maw!" I bark. "That ain't true. We'll get you up there, and then Nonc will come—he'll come and carry you back to the farm."

"Right," says Blackie. "Maybe I can tow you down this slough here and find a place where the bank ain't so steep."

Maw don't say nuttin' right away. I see her eyes lookin' around, and I hear her breathin' kinda hard. "It's OK, dogs," she says. "I 'preciate what you tryin' to do, but from what I seen, ole Uncle's gonna have to carry your boy back to the farm and that big ole coon dog what's on the other side, too. Nonc ain't a spry fella. And, anyway, he ain't gonna take no big snakebit cat outta the woods."

I'm 'bout to argue with Maw when I hear some yappin'— a bunch of dogs are comin', and they ain't far away. Soon the yappin' gets real loud, and before I know it a whole pack of dogs is standin' up on the bank lookin' down at us.

One of them is Sugarfoot!

"Sugarfoot! Sugarfoot!" I bark up at her. "Is Nonc here?"

She barks back, "Yes—well, no. He's not here yet, but he's comin' right behind, fast as he can."

"How far?" I say.

"I dunno, Rascal. Not far is all I can say."

"OK, well, we need some dogs to come down here to help Big Maw. She's been snakebit, and we gotta get her up this bank. Me and Blackie done tried, but we cain't do it ourselves."

I look up and there ain't a dog movin' a paw.

Then I hear one dog say, "What? You want us dogs to help that nasty ole cat?"

I'm 'bout to give this dog a good barkin' at when I hear Blackie speak up. "Y'all, this cat helped kill the snake that killed Mamou's baby, and she saved Rascal and his boy when she done it. She ain't the worst cat that ever lived. No, she ain't. She's hurtin', and we need to help her. C'mon, now. Y'all listen to Blackie. You know I wouldn't jive you 'bout no cat."

Them dogs are stuck like nails to the bank, shakin' their heads this way and then that way, all confused, till Sugarfoot yelps, "I'm comin', Mr. Blackie! I'm comin'!"

She dives down the bank.

Then there's a mudslide of dogs splashin' down in the water all around us.

I hear Big Maw say, "Now I know I'm dead, Rascal. Or elst I'm dreamin'."

"You ain't neither, Big Maw. Now hold on. Blackie, you'll take the scruff again?"

"Oh yeah," says Blackie. "I'm gettin' to where I like the taste of cat fur."

"Listen to him, Rascal—fresh ole hound. I cain't say I like the feel of his slobber."

I would laugh 'cept I see that Maw's hind leg's now swole up like a balloon.

Blackie latches on to Maw and I grab hold of her tail again, and the rest of the dogs get their noses under Maw's belly. We start pullin' and pushin' like crazy up the bank.

I hear dogs huffin' and puffin' and moanin' and groanin', and slowly but surely we've got Maw dragged almost to the top.

Then a shadow comes over us and I look up.

Nonc!

His ball cap is twisted sideways, his gun is in the crook of his arm, his face is all red and sweaty. He don't look happy.

He yells, "What kinda *roogarou* we got goin' on yuh,

ehn? Why y'all dogs chewin' on my cat? *Fais pas ça, chiens!*
Fais pas ça! Y'all let that cat go!"

Dogs are trained to listen, and almost every dog—even
me—jumps back, some of them tumblin' down the bank.

But Blackie don't. He digs in hard with his paws and
lunges forward, givin' one more tug with his head.

I watch as Maw rolls over onto the flat part of the bank.

Blackie stumbles up on the bank right after her, wet,
muddy, and whupped, and he slips and falls—just as Nonc
takes a kick at him.

"*Mauvais chien!*" he yells. "Bad dog. You kilt my cat!"

And every dog goes to howlin', "No! No! No!"

We see Blackie stagger to his feet and use what strength
he's got left to heave hisself outta the way of Nonc's second
kick.

Nonc's foot just finds air, and he almost tumbles over. He
lets out a long string of cusswords.

We see Blackie throw back his head and bawl.

Then he turns away and without makin' another sound
goes runnin' off hard into the swamp.

Chapter 17

We're up on the slough bank—me, my boy, and Nonc—lookin' down at Big Maw. She's a sad sight, muddy and wet, her gray and white fur plastered to her body. She ain't movin'.

She won't talk to me. I've even licked her, but she just lays there with her eyes shut. Her leg is blowed up bigger than ever.

I'm the only dog left 'cept for poor Mamou, who's still down there in the slough layin' on his side in the shallow water, his head up on a log. I can hear him groanin', low and pitiful: "Mamou's hurtin'—hurtin' bad, y'all. Somebody help me."

All them other dogs scattered when Nonc kicked at Blackie 'cause there ain't no dog wants to be around a dog-kickin', dog-cussin' man.

I wadn't gonna run away. I ran right up that bank and dodged around Nonc and went to my boy. Nonc finally saw him stuck out on that bridge and come over.

They had them a big drink of water out of a jug Nonc was carryin'. He gave my boy a piece of sugar candy 'cause Meely said he was feelin' weak.

Then Nonc chopped and chopped and chopped with that hatchet he brought along till he got my boy outta that hole.

While Nonc chopped, my boy told him what happened—how he'd gone all woozy and sleepy and woke up with that bad snake about to get him. He thought he was dreamin'.

He told how Big Maw jumped that snake and got herself bit and how Blackie jumped that snake, too.

Nonc kept shakin' his head.

My boy didn't even groan once while Nonc chopped him out, though I know it hurt 'cause I saw him make a face when Nonc pulled his leg from the thing that had it caught. An ole rusty spike, he said it was.

I tried to go lick my boy, but Nonc told me to get away, so I listened, though I didn't want to.

My boy had took off his outside shirt and stuffed it down that hole 'cause he'd been bleedin' bad.

Nonc said that shirt wadn't gonna be worn again by nobody, it was so bloody. So he ripped an arm off of it where it wadn't bloody and tied that arm around my boy's leg where it's hurt. He said that would stop the bleedin', but once we get out of these woods, my boy needs to go to a place called the hospital.

Nonc's lookin' around, puzzled.

"Well, that cat's done for," he says. "A snake that big's got poison enough to kill that bull in my pasture. We gonna have to leave her. When I come back for that broke-leg hound—Lawd knows how I'm gonna get him outta these woods—I'll bring a shovel and give the ole gal a proper burial. Lo-Lo liked that ole cat. I still don't understand what she was doin' way the heck out yuh. She almost never leaves that barn. Same wit' them dogs. How come they was all runnin' wild out yuh, too? Me, I'm confused."

I don't like what Nonc's sayin' 'bout Big Maw, and I bark to let him know.

He looks at me and says, all cross, "Shush. What you barkin' for, dog? I come found your boy like you wanted."

Meely's lookin' at Nonc like he don't like it, neither.

"I don't think she's dead, Mr. Voclain," says Meely. "I heard her mewlin' a coupla times just before you got here. It would be a shame to leave her like this if she's got a chance. She's a tough ole girl. She went after that snake even though she musta known he'd go after her."

Nonc looks down at Big Maw again, like he's aggravated. He nudges her, hard it seems to me, with his boot, but Maw still don't move.

"See, son? She's gone. She ain't a cat that would stand for that normally. She'd be tryin' to rip my boot off. Her time's done come. And, anyway, she must weigh thirty, forty doggone pounds. How I'm s'posed to carry her big self outta these woods and get you out, too, ehn? It's gettin' late, and you won't be able to go fast—heck, the shape you in, I might have to end up carryin' you. Then what I'm gonna do?"

"How 'bout if I carry her?" says Meely. "You could put her in my huntin' vest. I could—"

"Meely, you crazy? You look 'bout as whupped as that hound dog down there and you got a bum leg oozin' blood and you tellin' me you gonna carry this cat? C'mon, son. Henrietta's already catchin' a heart attack over this. She already tole me she don't like you traipsin' the woods all by yourself, and she's gonna put her foot down from now on. If we ain't outta here by dark, she's liable to call the doggone National Guard. Maybe she already has."

Meely looks down at Maw—a sad look. He nods. "I

understand. Here, help me bend down. I just wanna say goodbye to her. If not for her . . . well . . ."

Nonc's still aggravated, but he gives my boy an arm, and my boy bends down slow on his one good leg, holdin' his bad leg out. He makes a face when he does. He gets up close to Maw and tousles her wet, muddy head and whispers somethin' soft in her ear. Then he cradles her up in his arms and turns to Nonc.

"She's still warm, Mr. Voclain. And she really ain't all that heavy. Not really. Why don't you put her in my huntin' vest like I said and we'll see how far we get?"

Nonc lets out a big sigh. "Son, I know you like critters and Henrietta says you treat that dog like your brother, but we got us a serious situation. You need to get to a doctor quick, and if we get caught in these woods after dark, I ain't shore I can find my way out, not to mention that them *cousins* might come out and carry us away. When I come back wit' some help and if that cat really is alive, I'll bring her out—promise."

My boy holds Big Maw closer. "Well, don't worry 'bout gettin' lost," he says. "Me and Rascal here know the way back blindfolded. And since I cain't walk fast anyway, I might as well carry this cat."

Nonc looks down. His face is all sweaty, and he rubs it hard with his hands. "You hardheaded, son, you know that? OK, I'm gonna bend down. You put that cat in the back pouch of my huntin' vest, and then let's get outta yuh. Now, if Nonc drops dead of a heart attack before we get back to the truck, you gonna be sorry."

Meely nods. "I understand. Thank you, Mr. Voclain. Let's pack her up and see how far we get."

Nonc bends down beside my boy, who's tryin' to lift Maw toward the pack and still keep his balance. Nonc sees this ain't workin'.

"OK, move aside, I'll pick her up. You just guide her into the pouch."

This works better, and soon Maw's just a big lump in Nonc's vest.

Nonc stands and shakes his head. "Doggone, this cat musta ate a lotta my rats to get this fat."

He offers Meely a hand. Meely takes it and stands up, though he does it slow.

He makes a face like he's hurtin'.

"You need to hold on to me?" says Nonc. "If so, that's gonna really slow us down."

"No, sir. Let's just cut a sapling on the levee here and I'll use it as a walkin' stick."

"Now you talkin' some sense, son," says Nonc.

Chapter 18

We light out, goin' slow but not as slow as I expected we might. My boy has to stop pretty often. He's sweatin' good. So is Nonc.

They're thirsty and drink a lot of water. They ain't thought about givin' me none yet, but that's OK.

I walk out front most of the time, sniffin' high and low to make shore there ain't no more bad snakes about. Sometimes I fall behind to cover our backsides.

After a bit, a funny thing happens. First Sugarfoot comes trottin' up out of the woods beside me. She don't say a thing. She just nods.

Then, one by one, them other dogs that scattered when Nonc kicked at Blackie come out of the woods, and soon we got a whole pack of dogs walkin' with us, though Blackie ain't one of 'em.

Every dog wants to know where's the cat.

"In Nonc's sack," I tell 'em.

"Is she dead, Rascal?" asks Sugarfoot.

"I don't know," I say. "My boy thinks she ain't."

Nonc is lookin' around, puzzled again.

"Well, now look at this. We got us a whole army of dogs escortin' us outta the woods. Is it the full moon, Meely? I ain't never seen dogs carry on like this before."

"No, sir. The moon won't be full for another week."

We walk and walk and walk, stoppin' now and then, and

the light starts to fade fast when we hear some faint voices callin' out ahead. We all stop to listen.

Nonc calls back, but there ain't no answer.

But dogs hear a lot better than Two-Footers. I already know one of the voices.

It's Miz Henrietta!

I throw back my head and howl, and I tell all the other dogs to howl, too. Then I say to Sugarfoot, "Stay with my boy. I'm gonna go fetch these people!"

Nonc's yellin' for us to quiet down, but ain't no dog listenin' to him now.

I run fast, forgettin' that I'm beat, and come flyin' out of a palmetto thicket and all but stumble into a pile of people.

"Rascal!" one of them calls out. "Rascal, oh Lord, puppy. Where's Meely? Where's Nonc? Are they safe?"

I spy Miz Henrietta and go jumpin' up into her arms, forgettin' that I'm maybe the dirtiest dog ever. I lick her on the face and squeal. She stumbles backwards and drops me, but I don't fall hard.

I start jumpin' up and down. "Yes!" I bark. "Yes! My boy's close by!"

Then I go runnin' in Meely's direction, stoppin' quick and startin' again, yappin' the whole time so these people will understand.

"Follow him!" Miz Henrietta shouts out. "Follow that beagle!"

She's such a smart lady! I howl at this.

Two men, both wearin' funny tall hats, start runnin' my way. I slow down for them. When they catch up, I run at a Two-Footer's pace, barkin' and howlin' the whole way.

It don't take long before I hear 'em huffin' and puffin', but suddenly there's my boy and Nonc and Sugarfoot and all them other dogs.

I hear Nonc call out, "Thank Gawd y'all here. This boy's hurt—he's got a bum leg. He's all beat up and needs a doctor. And me, my back's about broke 'cause I'm carryin' this durn ole dead cat. C'mon, fellas, give us a hand."

The men in the hats rush over to Meely, and one of 'em says, "It's OK, son. We're gonna take care of you. C'mon, lean on me. We'll get you out of these woods and take you to the hospital and get you all fixed up."

And I'm jumpin' up and down barkin'—just barkin', barkin', barkin' 'cause I finally know my boy's gonna be OK. I hear Nonc tellin' me to pipe down, but I cain't.

And next I know Miz Henrietta's runnin' up and she's sayin', "Oh, Meely, oh, you poor, sweet boy, what's happened to you? Are you all right? I was so worried. I was—"

And I see Meely break free of that man and hobble toward Miz Henrietta, tossin' away his walkin' stick. He gives her a big hug. He says, his head tucked down on her shoulder, "Miz Lirette, I'm so sorry. I did a foolish thing back there and got myself stuck. I shoulda listened to Rascal, who tried to tell me not to cross that bridge. I'm so sorry. The last thing I ever wanted to do was worry you. I—"

But Miz Henrietta shushes him, not like Nonc shushes me, but real quiet. And I hear her say, in a whisper, "Meely, sweetie, it's OK. I'll be mad at you tomorrow, but right now I can only thank God that you're back. I don't know what I would've done if something had happened to you."

And they go quiet for a bit, and then I hear a sound and I know what it is.

My boy's cryin' and so is Miz Henrietta.

It's OK with me.

My boy's the bravest boy ever, but sometimes when you're done bein' brave and you don't have to be brave no more, all you can do is cry.

Me, I start cryin', too.

One of the men in the hats comes up and says, "We should get goin', Miz Lirette. That bandage around his leg has bled through. He should get looked after quick."

"Of course," says Miz Henrietta. "I'm deeply grateful, Sergeant Robichaux, that you and Sergeant Samanie came out. I can't thank you enough. Meely can ride with you, and I'll follow you in my car to the hospital."

We all turn to go when I hear Nonc speak up. "Well, Niece, what about me? You ain't got nuttin' to say to your ole uncle who's done traipsed all over creation to bring that boy back?"

"Oh, Nonc!" says Miz Henrietta. "Oh, Nonc—of course."

She breaks free from Meely and runs over to Nonc.

"Oh, poor, dear Uncle Noon," she says. "I'm so sorry. Of course—I can't thank you enough. You are the very best uncle in the world, and I'll never be able to repay you for this. Never."

She wipes some of them tears from her eyes and reaches out and hugs him.

I see Nonc nod and pat her on the back. "That's more like it, *cher*," he says. "But, no, you don't owe Nonc nuttin'. Meely's family to you, so he's family to me. That's how it works, you know."

"Oh, you are so sweet and kind, Uncle Noon," says Miz Henrietta as she pulls back and looks at him. "You look so hot and tired. Let me take some of your things. The deputies will help Meely out of the woods, and I'll help you."

Nonc shakes his head. "I don't need no help 'cept maybe that second fella could take this doggone cat off my back."

"A cat? What cat?"

"A big dead cat. That big gal cat that stays in my barn. She's in the pouch of my huntin' vest."

"A dead cat? I'm confused, Uncle Noon. Why do you have a dead cat?"

Meely speaks up.

"That cat saved my life—and Rascal's," he says. "And she might not be dead. It's complicated, Miz Henrietta, and I'll explain it all later. But maybe we could take the cat to the hospital, too? She was bitten by a snake. She—"

Nonc interrupts. "She's dead," he says. "But Meely, him, he wouldn't leave her behind. So Nonc yuh got to carry her. Must be five miles back to where I found 'em. That thing must weigh fifty pounds. Maybe sixty."

Now Miz Henrietta is really confused.

"Well, Meely, I don't think the hospital would take a cat," she says. "And if Nonc says she's dead, well—"

"I don't mean the real hospital," says Meely. "Maybe you could take her to Dr. Walters, the vet who takes care of Rascal. He'd know what to do. Please. We've come so far. It would be a shame—it—"

I see Nonc shake his head. "That boy's stubborn, Henrietta, but if you wanna take this cat to the vet, Nonc ain't got nuttin' to say about that. The onliest thing I know is that Nonc here cain't carry her one more foot. Nonc's beat as a Mardi Gras drum."

Miz Henrietta's lookin' down, like she's thinkin' what to do, then says, "Of course, Uncle. No one could expect you to do more than you've done already."

She looks at one of the men in the big hats and says, "Maybe you could take my uncle's vest? It's got a cat in it. It—"

"I heard," says the man. "And, yes, ma'am, I'll take it. Should I put it in your car?"

"Yes, that would be fine," says Miz Henrietta. "In the back-seat, I guess. Thank you, officer."

The man comes and collects Nonc's vest. He says, "Pod-nah, if there's a cat in there, that *is* some cat."

"I told you," says Nonc. "Biggest doggone cat on the face of the eart'."

We all turn to go and make it to the edge of the woods just as the last light is leavin' the sky. It's a good thing, too. I can hear them mosquitoes buzzin' down in droves from the trees. I'm thinkin' about poor Mamou back there in that slough. He'll do what dogs do. He'll just bury hisself in that soft mud till help comes.

Them deputies switch on some flashlights to shine the last part of the way. They open the door of their car and put my boy in the backseat.

I suddenly realize I need to go with him—he won't be happy without me.

I go boundin' up and jump between those deputies and into my boy's lap.

He laughs. "Oh, Rascal, you ole rascal, you. You are one

stinky dog, and we're gonna have to give you a proper bath tomorrow. But for now, you're gonna have to ride with Miz Henrietta. I'll see you again real soon, OK? Now, you jump down and go with her."

I'm whimperin' at that 'cause I don't want to leave him, but he gives me a nuzzle and then a li'l push, and I find myself hoppin' to the ground. I stand and look at him till Miz Henrietta comes over and leans in. She gives him a kiss on the cheek and says, "Meely, I'll meet you at the hospital. Once I know you're fine, I'll see if I can rouse Dr. Walters. But that's what we're going to do, so please don't argue with me. You could already have an infection setting in on that leg, and we need to take care of it, OK?"

"Yes, ma'am, I understand. Will Rascal ride with you?"

"No, I don't think that's a good idea. I'm going to ask Nonc to take Rascal home with him. Who knows how long we'll be, and that poor dog needs to get watered and fed."

I'm hearin' this and I don't like this, neither. I start to whimper again, but Miz Henrietta bends down and gives me a pat. "It's OK, puppy. I'm going to take good care of Meely, and we'll come fetch you in the morning."

She stands up and says to Nonc, "Is that OK, Nonc Noon? Would you mind taking Rascal for the night and we'll come for him in the morning?"

"Shore," says Nonc. "What's one more dog?"

He looks at me and all them other dogs and says, "C'mon, y'all. Hop in Nonc's truck. We goin' to the house. I'm hungrier than a spring alligator, and I bet y'all are, too. And I gotta call some of my podnahs to see if they'll help me go get big ole Mamou outta the woods."

He goes over, unlatches the tailgate to his truck, and opens it. *"Vien ici, chiens. Vien ici."*

All them dogs go runnin' for the truck 'cause after all the runnin' and walkin' they've done, they're happy to get a ride. But I ain't ready to go yet. I'm of a mind to try to follow them cars to town, though I don't know how far town might be.

But the other dog who ain't jumped in the truck is Sugarfoot. She comes up behind me and says, "C'mon, Rascal. Come to the farm. Your boy's gonna be fine now, and you look like a dog that could use some lickin', not to mention some food and water."

This could shore get a dog to thinkin', and I don't have to think long.

"OK, that sounds good—real good."

We trot over to the truck and jump up. Nonc shuts the tailgate behind us, goes around, and gets in. The engine sputters and rumbles to life.

Me and Sugarfoot put our paws up on the edge of the tailgate and look out. I see the car that's got Meely drive away, a

light flashin' on top of it, and I see Miz Henrietta get in her car and follow them.

Nonc waits till they're out of the way before he starts to turn his truck around.

I'm lookin' out, and in the very last light I see a dark shadow at the edge of the woods. I nudge Sugarfoot.

"Blackie?" she says.

I nod and bark out, "Blackie! Blackie, c'mon—we're all goin' to the farm!"

Blackie lifts his head and stares out toward the sound.

Then he lowers it, turns, and slinks off into the dark.

We ain't gone too far when Nonc's pickup slows down and stops. I hear him say, "Well, what's one *more* dog?"

He hops out of the truck and comes 'round. He shoos me and Sugarfoot back and opens the tailgate.

"Up you go," he says.

I look out—and it's my daddy, Tubby.

It takes his big, fat self three hops to make it up.

"Howdy, Rascal, son, I'm so pleased to see you," he says. "I tried to get here as quick as I could to help out, but you know a dog like me ain't used to the runnin' life. Did I miss a lot of excitement? I reckon I did. How you makin' out, puppy? Everything OK? You look tired as an ole tractor and muddy as Uncle Billy's hog. I'll bet you're hungry. Heck, I'm so hungry myself I could lick the silver off a spoon. How's the rest of you dogs? Everybody OK?"

I don't know why but I'm pleased to see Tubby even if he's got here late.

"Yes, you missed some excitement," I say, "but I'll tell you all about it at the farm. And I'm doin' good, Daddy—real good."

Chapter 19

Six months later . . .

It's a month my boy calls April on that day he calls Saturday. We're hikin' through the spring woods. It's mornin', not too early, warm but not yet hot.

There's a breeze stirrin' the cypress tops.

Some big ole puffy clouds are up in the sky.

I like lookin' at them clouds. Some of 'em look like bunnies to me. I've barked at a bunny cloud once or twice.

My boy gets a kick out of that.

Meely's goin' to catch him a mess of crawfish. He's given me a boiled crawfish to eat a time or two, and I like 'em. Meely's got a friend with him, Chickie.

He's fat and sweats a lot. He smells like a dog—well, somewhere 'tween a dog and a chicken and a cow. He's nice. He's got big, soft hands, and he gives me belly rubs all the time.

He tells my boy I'm the best dog ever. He wishes he had him a dog, but his momma won't get him a dog 'cause they got no money to feed a dog.

I don't know why they couldn't get a li'l dog that don't eat much. Chickie's a dog boy, just like my boy is, and any dog that got him for a boy would be a lucky dog.

After we got outta the woods that day, my boy had to spend the night in that hospital, and I was lonesome and worried, even though I stayed at Nonc's and had lots of dog company.

When I finally dozed off, I slept like a dead dog, pretty

much slept the night and day away till Miz Henrietta come to pick me up. I was so stiff and sore that I walked to Miz Henrietta's car like a pokey ole man.

But when we drove up and I saw my boy out on the front porch waitin' for me, I forgot I was stiff and sore. I jumped outta the window of Miz Henrietta's car—I didn't care that it was still movin'. I run up and jumped in his arms and almost knocked him over.

We had us a good, long nuzzle.

Then my boy put me down and reached in his shirt pocket and took somethin' out.

It was a medal with my name on it. He put it on my collar. He read it. It said "Rascal, Bravest Dog Ever."

Then he give me a bath with the hosepipe over by the cistern. I don't like baths normally, but I didn't mind this one.

Boy, I got soapy! I smelled good, my boy said!

The crawfish place he's got in mind is far, in the same stretch of woods where he got stuck on that bridge, but not all the way to that bridge, so Chickie's come along. If I never see that bridge again, it's all right with me. They've got a big burlap sack to put the crawfish in and crawfish nets and some bait—smelly chicken necks that Miz Henrietta give 'em from the icebox.

We walk and walk and walk, not too fast 'cause Chickie don't walk fast, and I like it. There's lots to sniff—mushrooms and toadstools and flowers and dandelions everyplace, not to mention trails where them rabbits have walked. I've hit a hot track now and then, and I give a li'l bark when I do—it just comes out. But it ain't bunny season and I'm stickin' with my boy.

We finally come to a swamp levee, and my boy climbs up and says to Chickie, "This is the place. Nonc Noon says he caught a whole sack of crawfish here last year. Let's bait up our nets."

Me and Chickie ramble on up to the top of the levee, and I look out at the swamp. It's nice—mossy cypresses with them knees pokin' up everyplace, and a cluster of flowers my boy calls swamp irises. I hear some birds tweedlin' out in the distance. The water is shallow and dark and smells old.

That's how them crawfish like it.

The sun's pokin' down in between them treetops. I can see myself in the reflection of that water.

I look OK. I'm a grown dog now—big for a beagle, like everybody said I was gonna be. I'm taller than my daddy, Tubby, even though he's got pure blood. It's that bluetick in me.

My boy and Chickie go about baitin' them nets. I watch for a while, then find some soft grass in a warm patch of sunlight and lay myself down. I laze around in that warm grass, snoozin' on and off. I hear Chickie squeal now and then when them nets come up full of crawfish.

I don't muss with crawfish much, though I'll bark at the ones that sometimes slip out of the net and try to crawl back into the swamp. One time I got too close to a big ole crawdad, and he latched onto my nose with them claws of his.

I run up and down the levee tryin' to throw that thing off, my boy runnin' after me hollerin' and laughin'.

I didn't think it was funny. I ain't got too close to a crawfish since.

I go up to my boy for a pat. He's stooped down on the levee

lookin' out at the swamp, and he gives me a good one. Chickie says he wants some dog love, too, so I go over and we rassle 'round for a while. It's fun. He likes to play dead, and I have to lick him on the face to get him to come alive. He laughs a lot, Chickie does.

Then Meely says it's time to check the nets again, so Chickie goes over to help.

I decide to wander down the levee bank a ways, seein' what I might sniff up. Plenty of critters have walked this levee.

I pick up the scent of bunnies, coons, and even the faint smell of a deer. It's all old, though.

I'm just out of sight of my boy when I pick up another smell that makes my hackles rise—snake!

I'm 'bout to bark when I hear a voice I've heard before.

"So how you makin' out, Rascal? Look at you—all grown up."

I turn.

It's Ole Swamp.

He's coiled up hard against the crook of a cypress tree. He's starin' at me, not movin' a muscle, not even his tongue.

"It's OK," he says. "We're friends, remember? Well, OK, not friends. We're just not enemies."

I find myself backin' away—I just cain't help it.

"Rascal, really now. I thought we were over all this."

I stop. It's true: if Ole Swamp was gonna bite me, I'd already be bit.

He keeps talkin'. "Look, I appreciate what you done—tellin' them mutts they had treed the wrong snake. Oh, I coulda waited 'em out, but it woulda messed up my plans for the day. So, c'mon, tell me. How you doin'?"

I look good at Swamp. He seems bigger than I remember him, though not as big as Pick.

"I'm fine," I say. "How 'bout you?"

"Nice of you to ask. I'm good. Had me a nice, long snooze through the winter, and I woke up feelin' real good—better still when I remembered that your pals put a whuppin' on Pick. I'da never believed such a thing, but I saw it with my own eyes—well, at least I saw Pick floatin' broke-neck in that slough. It couldn'a happened to a nicer fella. I'm only sorry I didn't get to see him go down, but I was, well, you know, held up by them dogs, and I wadn't too keen to come out 'fore I knew they were all gone."

I nod.

I've had bad dreams about what Pick almost done to my boy, and what he done to Mamou and Big Maw, and it ain't a thing I care to talk about.

"I'm sorry 'bout what happened to that cat," Swamp goes on. "I know she wadn't fond of snakes, but I have a sweet spot for her now."

I nod at that, too. I look close at Swamp, wonderin' what he knows. I don't know what to say to that, either.

"It's OK, Rascal. I know some things are hard to talk about. Anyway, y'all dogs don't have to worry 'bout snakes any- more—well, *my* snakes, at least. I've gone out and whipped all of Pick's renegades and got 'em back into line. We're done with farmhouses. Us cottonmouths and our brother copper- heads are gonna live wild off these woods the way a snake's supposed to live or we won't live at all. You can tell all them dogs that."

"What about them rattlesnakes?" I say.

"Good point. I ain't in charge of them. But there ain't that many of 'em in this low country. 'Course, I've told 'em what I think, but that don't mean they'll listen. Like you know, there's good snakes and bad snakes, same as there's good dogs and bad dogs."

I cain't disagree with that.

We go silent for a bit. Then Swamp says, "How's your boy? Sounded like he'd busted up his leg pretty bad."

I still don't like Swamp axin' 'bout my boy, but I know it's easier just to answer. "He's good. He got better quick. We've got back to huntin'. Today, we're crawfishin'. He's brought a friend, Chickie. They're just down the bank there."

"I know. I heard y'all when y'all come up. I just have one question, Rascal. Answer me this—why'd he do it?"

"Why did who do what?"

"Why did your boy save my life that day? What's a snake to a boy?"

I gotta think about this.

Then I say, "Well, 'cause he's a good boy, I guess. 'Cause he thinks all critters have a place in the woods."

I look at Ole Swamp and smile.

I say, "Even snakes."

I didn't know snakes could smile, but Swamp smiles back. "What you meant to say was 'Especially snakes,' now didn't you, Rascal?"

I nod. "Yes, sir, that's gotta be what I meant."

Swamp shakes his head. "You better watch out, doggy. You could give dogs a good reputation."

I find myself laughin' at this.

"Well," says Swamp, "I gotta go. I've got a certain frog

on my mind that I hope will become friends with my stomach. Now, I could stay and gab a bit longer if you want to trot back up the levee and bring Ole Swamp a few of them crawfish your boy's catchin'. Them things are a bit hard to swallow but real tasty after you get 'em down."

I nod. "I've had 'em myself, peeled, but I don't like to muss with them live ones. But good luck with that frog, Swamp."

"OK," says Swamp. "See you, Rascal. You look after yourself, son. And don't be a stranger."

I stand still and watch him unwind his big self before I turn to go. I guess I still don't trust snakes completely. He slithers off the levee and heads out, sidewindin' slow across the water.

I'm glad I'm not that frog.

I trot on back to my boy and Chickie. I'm happy just to laze about while they fill up that sack with crawfish. Soon Meely says they've got all they can carry and we should head on home.

We make our way slow back to the edge of the woods and come out to a headland cuttin' through a cornfield. We walk and walk and walk and walk along that headland till we reach Miz Henrietta's. I'm tired and happy to be home.

Meely says to Chickie, "I'm gonna go in and tell Miz Henrietta we're back. You take the crawfish over to the hosepipe out behind the cistern and start washin' 'em off. There's a big ole washtub leanin' up against the house there. Just dump 'em all in that. I'll come out in a few minutes to help you."

"OK," says Chickie.

My boy turns to me. "C'mon up to the porch, Rascal. I'll get you a dog biscuit from the kitchen."

I bark at that!

My boy goes in and comes out quick. I do my usual biscuit dance, and he tosses me that treat. It ain't the best throw Meely's ever made, but I jump and catch it clean over my shoulder.

"Rascal, you're too much! You oughta play center field for my softball team!" my boy says.

He comes over and gives me a pat and skips off the porch to go help Chickie. I'll go see them crawfish later.

I wanna see how everybody else is doin'.

I head out to the big backyard toward the li'l barn. It's a shed really.

A carpenter friend of Miz Henrietta come over, about the time the weather got cold, and built it. I watched it go up, though it was noisy when the man did it—all that hammerin' and sawin'.

He built it out of a wood called cedar. It smells awfully good. The shed looks pretty much like the barn in Nonc Noon's pasture, 'cept real small. The man put in a wood floor and Meely dragged in a coupla bales of hay and spread some of it around.

I get close and bark out, "Anybody home?"

"Hey, Rascal, sugar," says a voice from inside. "Y'all back already? Get your doggy self in here."

I go in the double doors. The man put a big ole window at the back of the barn. It's open. There's a nice breeze stirrin' and the sun's streamin' in, makin' a spotlight on about half the floor.

I see Big Maw layin' up on a bale of hay, enjoyin' that sunshine.

"Hey, Big Maw, how you doin'?"

"She's doin' all right for a three-legged cat," says another voice.

I look over and there's Blackie curled up in a corner.

"Oh, hey, Blackie, I didn't know you were here."

"Oh, I'm here. You think I could go off and ramble and leave this poor ole crippled cat to laze around here all day by herself? She'd be bored stiff."

Big Maw stretches and yawns. "Would you listen to him, Rascal. He's layin' around up in here 'cause ain't a dog on earth likes to talk more than he does—well, 'cept maybe Tubby. You know how many times I've heard his nootra-huntin' stories? Well, count the *tchoupique* in that bayou across the road and it's about that many times."

"I thought you liked my nootra-huntin' stories."

Maw smiles. "I didn't say I didn't like 'em. I was just tellin' Rascal how many times you've told 'em."

"Well, you liked it when I used my best nootra-huntin' move on that snake," says Blackie.

"Yes, I did. And every time I tell that snake story to my cat podnahs, I go outta my way to say, 'Ole Blackie—yeah, believe it or not, *that* Blackie, that ole mange-rug, bit-eared, fleabag hound dog—he come outta nowhere and broke that snake's neck quicker than Big Maw kills a rat.' I tell 'em just like it happened."

Maw smiles.

"Well, you could leave out the part about 'mange-rug, bit-eared, and fleabag' next time," says Blackie.

Maw chortles. "I could, Blackie, but a cat's gotta testify to the doggone truth."

Blackie looks at me. "See what I gotta put up wit'?"

Maw stands and stretches on her three good legs. "I don't s'pose you caught me a rat out there, did you, Rascal? Boy, I shore got me an *envy* for a nice, juicy rat. Now, don't get me wrong—this store-bought food the lady brings me is plenty good. But there ain't nuttin' better than a big, fat rat, no way."

"No, ma'am. We didn't run across no rats, but I'll keep lookin' for 'em every time we go out there."

"Well, that's awfully nice of you."

"I told her I would bring her a nootra," says Blackie. "Them things is just big ole rats is all. But she's particular, that lady."

"Blackie," says Maw, "a nootra ain't a rat, even if them Cajuns call 'em nootra-rats. You drug one in the yard and I smelled it, and it don't smell nuttin' like a rat. I'm not sayin' if I was starvin' I wouldn't eat on a nootra. But a cat ain't like a dog, eatin' everything that falls dead."

"That's not true," says Blackie. "I wouldn't eat no buzzard if it fell dead right in front of me."

"Well, that's good to know," says Maw, " 'cause if you ate a buzzard, you wouldn't be sleepin' in Maw's barn, no way."

Blackie shakes his head. "Hear that, Rascal? That lady's hard. Hard, I'm tellin' ya."

"Maw ain't hard. A cat's gotta have standards, Rascal. That's just how it is. A cat ain't like a dog, no, it ain't."

She looks at me. "Well, *some* dogs is what I mean."

Then Blackie and Maw have themselves a belly laugh.

Maw come to live with us after she decided she wadn't gonna die.

Miz Henrietta carried her to that vet, Dr. Walters, after she took my boy to the hospital. Meely was right—Maw was alive, though barely. The doctor said she was in somethin' called shock from that snake poison, and he didn't have much hope for her. He said her leg was ruined and she wouldn't be able to use it ever again. He didn't think she'd live the night.

But she did and the next night and the next and lots of nights after that. She just laid there in that shock, barely breathin'.

Then her leg got rotten, and the doctor said he needed to cut some of it off. But he thought maybe it would just be better to put her to sleep for good.

My boy didn't want to hear that.

But Miz Henrietta told Meely that doctor might be right, that puttin' her to sleep might be the best thing for Maw 'cause a cat as wild as her might not wanna live crippled.

My boy said he understood all that but thought it would be a shame since Big Maw had fought that snake poison all this time.

If she wadn't quittin', nobody should quit on her.

Miz Henrietta thought that over. "Well, OK, but, Meely, if she makes it, you'll have to take care of her."

And my boy said, "Does that mean she'll come to live with us?"

And Miz Henrietta said it probly would be best—that a three-legged cat might not have such a good time of it tryin' to get by on Nonc's farm.

The doctor took part of that leg, and Maw laid up for a good while longer. But she got better.

She come home in a big cardboard box that my boy toted from the backseat of Miz Henrietta's car. He took Maw out of that box and carried her up to the big front porch and put her down.

She looked around, confused for a bit, till she saw me. She smiled, though she looked tired.

I went runnin' up and give her a big lick, I was so happy to see her.

"Why am I here, Rascal?" she wanted to know. "How come I'm not back at the barn wit' my boys?"

I didn't think I should tell her that Nonc might not want her no more. So I told her I didn't know, but I was glad she was here.

I guess she figgered it out anyway.

She lived in the house at first and moped about, draggin' herself here and there on her three good legs. The longer she stayed, the stronger she got, and when the weather got nice again, Meely started lettin' her out in the yard.

Once Maw got out there, she didn't want to go back in the house. She liked goin' over and layin' up under Miz Henrietta's flower bushes.

She'd lay there real still, just watchin' the world go by. Sometimes, though, some critter would come by that didn't know Maw was there. She'd go after 'em, even though her missin' leg had caused her to lose her spring.

She even got a bird in her paws once.

She talked about that bird for days and days and days. "Oh, Rascal, I could almost taste that bird," she would tell me. "That'a been somethin' if ole Maw caught that bird. I ain't given up on catchin' one, you know."

Maw was so happy bein' outside that she quit mopin'.

It was Meely's idea to build that shed in the yard so Maw could come and go as she pleased. It was his idea to have the man build it like Nonc's barn. He paid for it outta money he made doin' chores for Miz Henrietta and other people.

Maw loves her li'l barn, even though I know she misses her boys and chasin' Nonc's rats. Sometimes my boy puts her back in that box and takes her for a visit over there. Her boys have grown up and give them rats fits.

Blackie come to us later.

He wouldn't go back to Nonc's—he decided he'd live wild before he'd go back to a dog-kickin' man.

I understood that, but I felt like my boy felt—that Nonc, well, he ain't perfect but he ain't the worst fella ever. He did get my boy off that bridge and outta the woods, same as Maw, and he and some fellas did go back the next day and rescue Mamou. They pushed him in a wheelbarrow clear outta them woods.

Nonc took him to the doctor and got his hip fixed up like new.

Mamou's gone back to chasin' them deer—though Nonc still ain't caught one.

One time I visited Nonc's with my boy, and Mamou actually talked to me. He invited me over to meet Bon-Bon and them puppies. Me and Bon-Bon talked 'bout Momma for a good long time.

I heard all about my faraway bluetick family.

I guess I've changed my mind about deer dogs.

At first, Blackie showed up to Miz Henrietta's just for a visit. He didn't look so good—skinny and all. Wadn't nobody home the first time but me and Maw. I was up on the porch when I saw him come in the yard. Maw was in her barn.

I barked to him, and he come over. We talked, and I told him 'bout Maw bein' here—he didn't even know she was alive. I said he should go say hello.

"You think she really wants to see me, Rascal?"

I said I thought she did.

He went over there and barked out from the door. Maw come on out. She said, "Well, look what the cat dragged in."

She had herself a belly laugh over that.

Blackie laughed, too.

She invited him in, and they had themselves a good visit. Maw even give him the rest of her cat food she had left over. She told him to come back sometime. He said he would.

He come back later, on that day my boy calls Sunday, when everybody was here. Meely saw him first and called him over.

"Poor Blackie," I heard him say. "You're skin and bones, pooch. C'mon to the porch. I'll get you some of Rascal's food."

Blackie followed a good ways behind my boy—I guess he wadn't shore if this was a good idea. He didn't know who else might be there, and he didn't want to be kicked at no more.

He looked at me, and I smiled. I told him it was OK, he wadn't gonna get kicked here. I was glad he was gettin' some of my food—I had plenty.

Later, Miz Henrietta come out on the porch. Blackie had ate all that food, and me and him was just lazin' up there in a sunny patch shootin' the breeze. He told me he'd roam all the way up to the garbage dump in town to find his supper some nights.

One time he found a T-bone steak, though it had been ate some by the person who threw it away, and it wadn't the freshest.

But I could tell livin' wild was hard on Blackie. His eyes were dull. He said his guts hurt worse than ever.

Miz Henrietta called out to Meely to ask him about this new dog. Meely told her what he knew about Blackie. He said Blackie was brave and smart and a lot better dog than Nonc thought he was, but he had never had anybody to really look after him good.

She said, "Poor thing. Maybe we should bring him to the pound. Maybe a good family would adopt him."

"I doubt that," Meely said. "He's not a pretty dog, and he's not so young anymore. At the pound, they'd just put him to sleep. I think he's better off wild—unless we want to take him in."

Miz Henrietta shook her head. "You're the sweetest boy ever, Meely, but we can't keep taking in strays. We can't."

My boy said he understood that—though I don't think he did.

Blackie went off, but he kept comin' back ever so often. Meely would feed him, or Maw would give him some of her food. He never asked for the food, and he always said thank you.

Sometimes he'd go wanderin' our yard—it's a big yard. Once he run into a snake at the back end. It wadn't a poisonous snake, but Blackie chased it off.

Meely saw what Blackie did and told Miz Henrietta. She don't like snakes, and I could tell she was glad.

One day we were out on the porch—me, Maw, Meely, and Miz Henrietta—when Blackie wandered in from the backyard. Miz Henrietta was sittin' in her rockin' chair, readin' a book. Blackie come right up on the porch, not sayin' a word. He went over slow to Miz Henrietta and just stood there lookin' at her.

Lookin' and lookin' and lookin'.

Finally, she looked up.

"Well, hello, Blackie. Back again?" she said.

Blackie waggled his big ole long tail and then went up and put his head in her lap—just like that.

"Ohhh," Miz Henrietta groaned, though she didn't groan in the worst way.

She pushed Blackie away, but not hard.

She said, "Blackie, no, no. You're a dirty old dog. You need a bath. You need a flea collar. You need—"

Blackie just looked up at her with his big, sad eyes and nodded.

She shook her head and then give Blackie a pat on the head.

Miz Henrietta looked at my boy. "Meely, did you put this dog up to this?"

My boy smiled. "No, ma'am. He's just a good-hearted lonesome ole dog who knows a good person when he sees one."

Miz Henrietta shook her head. "A pushover, you mean. OK, Emile LaBauve. If we take this dog in, he's your responsibility, like the rest of these critters. And that's it—no more. No more dogs, no more cats, no more pets of any kind. Is that a deal?"

My boy jumped up and ran over and hugged Miz Henrietta so hard he almost knocked her out of her rockin' chair. "Oh, this is so nice of you. And, yes, of course, I'll take care of him. And I promise—no more pets."

Then he give Blackie a big ole pat on the head and said, "C'mon, boy. Let's get you somethin' to eat."

"You need to give that dog a bath. And then schedule an appointment with the vet to get him checked over."

"Yes, ma'am."

I could tell Blackie didn't think much of the bath part—he'd never had one before. But he wadn't gonna argue.

Then we raced off that porch, my boy yellin', me and Blackie barkin' and barkin' and barkin'.

That's how we come to be a family here. We're a jambalaya of a family, but a family just the same.

Maw didn't have much to say. She didn't want to let on that she liked Blackie in front of my boy. But I knew she was pleased.

Funny things have happened. Miz Henrietta said Blackie would be Meely's dog, just like I am, but she's took a shine to that ole hound. She bought him a fancy collar with his name on it and a flea collar, too. She's the one who took him to the doctor and got his worm medicine.

Once them worms got out of his guts, Blackie become the sweetest dog ever. I ain't heard him say a cross word since.

Miz Henrietta's the one who gives him his dog biscuits.

She even lets him in the house now and then.

Blackie tries to do his part to be a good dog. I could patrol the yard, but I let Blackie do it. He feels better if he has a job.

A few times a day, he goes out and sniffs all around for snakes and such. Strangers don't set a foot in the yard without Blackie out there raisin' a racket.

It took him a while to stop barkin' at the mailman. He did only 'cause Miz Henrietta got cross at him 'cause, like all them dogs at Nonc's, he just don't like the mailman. He listens to her good.

Him and Maw are a pair—they lay up in the barn or out on the porch yakkin' and snoozin' and yakkin' and snoozin'. The way they sometimes crab at each other, you'd think they weren't friends. But I've seen 'em a lotta times curled up together, Maw with her big head on Blackie's soft belly.

Goes to show—you never know about dogs and cats.

Blackie and Maw remind me of Nonc Noon and Tante Lo-Lo.

Not too long ago, my boy took me and Maw back for a visit to Nonc's. He set Maw down in the barn, and she went over to see her boys. They'd caught a rat—boy, was Maw happy!

She ate her share and smacked her lips like my boy does when he eats ice cream.

Sugarfoot come over to see me. Oooh, she was glad to see me. Oooh, she smelled so good—different than she'd ever smelled.

We sniffed and rolled around all frisky.

We were happy, happy, happy!

It was better than chasin' bunnies!

We went home and Miz Henrietta was sittin' on the front porch when we got there. She wanted to know how it was at Nonc's.

My boy said, "Well, Maw had a fine time, and ole Rascal here *really* had a good time."

"How so, Meely?"

"You know that beautiful little black girl dog with the white foot? The one they call Sugarfoot?"

"Yes, I think I remember that dog."

"Well, I think she's gonna be a momma and Rascal's gonna be a daddy."

"What!?" Miz Henrietta said.

"Yes, ma'am."

"Are you sure?"

"Well, there's a good chance. And I was thinkin' about it, Miz Lirette. Can you imagine how beautiful their puppies will be? I can't wait to see—"

Miz Henrietta stopped him. "Emile LaBauve, I hope you're not suggesting what I think you might be suggesting? There's no way we're going to take in a puppy, though I'm sure Rascal's puppies will be beautiful."

And my boy looked at her all serious and said, "Of course, no, ma'am. A deal's a deal, and I wouldn't dream of askin' you to take in a puppy—unless you really wanted to."

And then my boy threw back his head and laughed.

And Miz Henrietta just looked at him like she was cross, until he run over to her and hugged her like crazy, and then she laughed, too.

And I threw back my head and howled—howled like the happiest dog that God ever let live.

ACKNOWLEDGMENTS

To **Nathaniel Brooks Horwitz** for his discerning critique and good advice; and to his mom and dad, **Geraldine Brooks** and **Tony Horwitz,** for making him available as an early reader.

To **Carrie Hannigan** at Russell & Volkening for placing *Rascal* in the kindly hands of **Erin Clarke** at Knopf's Young Readers Group; and to Erin for her thoughtful and deft editing of the manuscript.

Finally, to my late parents, **Rex** and **Bonnie Wells,** who gave me a childhood in the country filled with dogs and cats.

AUTHOR'S NOTE

Rascal begins his life on the bayouside farm of Noon and Lo-Lo Voclain, a Cajun couple in their seventies. The farm is set in the rural low country of southeast Louisiana. Sugarcane is grown by the hundreds of thousands of acres on the high ground. Much of the region, however, sits at sea level, a vast and wild apron of woodlands, marshes, and swamps fanning out to the Gulf of Mexico.

It's a wonderful place for a dog and his boy to ramble.

Hundreds of acres of sugarcane fields surround the Voclain farm, where the Voclains, like many small Cajun farmers, keep a few head of cattle and flocks of chickens, and grow vegetables, including okra, which is prized as an ingredient in the gumbos they make.

The road that runs by the farm is a winding farm road typical of that part of the country. There is no rock in low-lying south Louisiana, and roadbeds were made from available material—in most cases, clam or oyster shells dredged up from nearby lakes.

The Cajuns are Louisiana's best-known ethnic group, famed for their upbeat music accented by accordions and fiddles and sung in French. Their delicious, spicy dishes—gumbo, jambalaya, and crawfish, to name a few—are now being cooked in homes and restaurants around the globe.

But who are they?

The Cajuns descend from French settlers who migrated from northern France in the seventeenth century to what was then the French-held eastern coastal Canadian province of Acadia (today known as Nova Scotia). When the British gained control of Acadia in the mid-eighteenth century, the Acadians' lands were seized and they were forced into exile at sea.

After much hardship—hundreds of Cajuns perished or were sent to labor camps in the Caribbean—many ended up on the remote, sparsely settled south Louisiana coast, which was then part of France's vast holdings in the New World. Over time, the term *Acadian* became shortened to *'Cadian* and finally to *Cajun*.

The Cajuns of old spoke a perfectly fine if antique form of country French. That language, today called Cajun French, still survives in pockets, although the vast majority of Cajuns now speak English as their first language.

As the Cajuns underwent their slow transition from French speakers to English speakers, many began to talk in mixed sentences—a phrase of Cajun followed by a phrase of English (or they would drop into the middle of an English sentence a French word that they thought better captured the point they were trying to make or the thing they were trying to describe). This is a common trait among ethnic groups settling in a new land and learning a new language.

Many also spoke English with a singular accent. Some still do, although these days, when even the most remote Cajun enclaves have access to the homogenized English broadcast on 24/7 cable TV, the Cajun accent is fading. One trait of the accent, for example, is to obliterate the soft *h* in English words. A Cajun with a heavy accent will say "wit'" instead of "with" and "t'anks" instead of "thanks." This is not a mark of ignorance but simply the way the brain and palate of some Cajun speakers process certain English words. I've tried to capture the spirit of that in the dialect used in this book.

A GLOSSARY OF CAJUN TERMS AND EXPRESSIONS AND A GUIDE TO PRONUNCIATIONS

bayou (BY-yoo): A small, winding, slow-moving creek or river often meandering through a swamp or marsh. Also: a settlement. Many Cajun pioneers built their houses along the banks of bayous, which were the only natural high ground in their marshy low country. Bayous also served as the primary arteries of transportation in a place where roads scarcely existed or were hard to build. Over time, Cajuns living along a certain bayou began to think of themselves as part of a unified community. Today, a modern Cajun might tell you, "I live on Bayou Black," even if he resides in a house built in a subdivision miles away from the actual bayou bank.

beaucoup (BO-coo): Many.

beb: Babe or honey. A term of endearment.

bulleye: A battery-operated light mounted on a strap that can be worn around the head like a miner's light, allowing a hunter to shine for game hands-free. The act of hunting at night with a bulleye is called bulleyeing.

cane knife: A type of machete whose main feature is a sharp hook or grabber at its tip that is used to pick up cut sugarcane.

cayenne (KY-yan): The Cajuns' favorite cooking pepper.

cher: Dear. In Cajun French, pronounced *sheh*.

chien: Dog.

Chiens couillons! Chiens fous! Vous n'avez pas le sentiment que vous êtes né avec!: Idiot dogs! Crazy dogs! You don't have the sense you were born with!

couillon (coo-YAWN): Idiot or idiotic.

cousins (coo-ZENZ): French for "cousins" but used by Cajuns as a regionalism for mosquitoes.

craque (crock-KAY): Someone who has cracked up; crazy.

crawfish: Crayfish. A small freshwater crustacean prized by Cajuns for the pot. Crawfish boils, held mostly in the spring and summer, are festive occasions at which families and friends gather around steaming mounds of crawfish cooked in a variety of spicy concoctions.

ehn: The Cajun equivalent of "huh?" or "what?"

envy (awhn-VEE): A craving; a hankering to do something.

Fais pas ça (FAY pah sah): Don't do that.

frissons (free-SOHNZ): Chills; a sensation of fright.

gumbo: A spicy soup, traditionally served over rice, made with chicken, sausage, or seafood, and often containing okra. (In fact, the term *gumbo* comes from the central African word for okra.) Traditional gumbos start with a roux, which is simply flour browned in cooking oil.

headland: A narrow dirt road, often covered in grass and running through sugarcane fields, used primarily to allow tractors and harvesters access to the fields but wide enough to accommodate pickup trucks.

jambalaya (jum-buh-LY-yuh): A staple dish of rice, chicken or seafood, and spices. It's similar to paella, which is popular in Spanish cooking.

johnsongrass: An invasive, perennial weed that grows in tall, dense clumps. It provides nice cover for wildlife but is a pest in fields and gardens.

Lawd, 'Ti' Claude: Literally, "Oh Lord, Little Claude." The expression, common to the bayous of southeast Louisiana, is equivalent to "my oh my" or "oh man."

levee: A natural or man-made ridge along a bayou or waterway. Artificial levees, such as those along the Mississippi River, serve as flood-protection barriers.

loup garou (loop gah-ROO): The Cajun version of the werewolf. Often pronounced *roogarou*.

mais (may): But.

Mauvais chien! (mo-VAY shee-ehn): Bad dog.

nonc (nonk): Uncle.

nootra: Properly, the nutria (NOO-tree-uh), a beaver-sized South American rodent introduced into the Louisiana coastal marshes in the 1950s to increase the region's fur production. The animal has since become a pest, muscling out the smaller muskrat from its native territory. Nutrias are widely blamed for grazing practices that destroy marsh grass and flood-protection levees.

palmetto: A low-growing wild palm featuring broad fronds and berries, also known as the saw palmetto. Palmettos often grow in dense, almost impenetrable stands called brakes.

parish: The Louisiana equivalent of a county.

pirogue (PEE-roag or PEE-roh): A small wooden boat that is the Cajun equivalent of a canoe.

roseau **cane** (ROH-zoh): An aquatic reed growing in dense clusters along bayou banks or in the marsh. Known elsewhere as giant reedgrass.

satsuma: A type of cold-tolerant mandarin orange commonly grown in south Louisiana.

tante (taunt): Aunt.

tchoupique (shoe-pick): A primitive bony fish, also known as the bowfin, common to swampy waters.

'ti' (tee): Small or little; a shortening of the French word *petit*. It is common in the Cajun belt for the youngest or smallest son in a family to wear 'Ti' as part of his nickname, as in 'Ti' Joe or 'Ti' Fred.

Venez ici, mon cher petit chien: Come here, my sweet little dog.

Well, I'll be John Brown: An exclamation of surprise.

NAME PRONUNCIATIONS

Cancienne: CON-see-ann
Daigle: DAY-gull
LaBauve: luh-BOVE (rhymes with *cove*)
Lirette: LEE-rhet
Naquin: NOCK-ehn
Voclain: VO-clehn

KEN WELLS grew up on the banks of Bayou Black, in South Louisiana's Cajun country, on a farm where he and his five brothers romped with a dozen or so mostly adopted dogs, including a spectacular beagle named Tootie, and a goodly number of barn cats. For a while, his family even kept a pet monkey.

Wells, a career journalist, is the author of six previous books, including *Meely LaBauve,* a coming-of-age story that was an American Library Association Best Book for Young Adults. Wells lives in New York City with his wife, Lisa Newmark. They have two grown daughters, Sara and Rebecca.

GEORGE RODRIGUE (cover artist) was born and raised in New Iberia, Louisiana, the heart of Cajun country. Using the oak tree as his subject in hundreds of paintings in the early 1970s, Rodrigue eventually expanded his oeuvre to include the Cajun people and their traditions, as well as his interpretations of myths such as Jolie Blonde and Evangeline. It was one of these legends, the loup-garou, that inspired Rodrigue's most famous series, the Blue Dog, which became an international pop icon and catapulted the artist to worldwide fame. Rodrigue is the author of ten books and owns and operates three galleries. In 2009, Rodrigue founded the George Rodrigue Foundation of the Arts to support and encourage the use of visual arts in school curricula and art education programs. He lives with his wife, Wendy, in New Orleans.

CHRISTIAN SLADE carried his sketchbook everywhere he went as a boy growing up in New Jersey. It was said that he sometimes lived in another world, and it was this other world within the pages of his sketchbook that inspired him to draw from his imagination and the world around him. After thirty years, not much has changed. A former Disney animator and currently a full-time freelance illustrator, Slade is the creator of the graphic novel series Korgi. He is also the illustrator of *The Daring Adventures of Penhaligon Brush* and *The Curse of the Romany Wolves* by S. Jones Rogan and *Sunshine Picklelime* by Pamela Ferguson. Slade lives in Florida with his wife, their toddler twins, and two Welsh corgis.